Thirty Scarves

Epilogue:

It was another high school day at Pleasantville High School. She tripped getting off the bus and walked into school with a bright red face. She was so embarrassed, and she hoped no one saw—especially not John.

There he was, walking down Lincoln Hall. He was surrounded by all his friends and he looked so carefree. She liked that about him. He always looked happy, like he knew a joke no one else did. Plus, he was nice to look at. He was tall and confident—handsome and funny. She had had a crush on him since she had first seen him in elementary school, even if she didn't know it then.

He saw her trip and he laughed softly. He thought it was cute how fast she walked to class. He wondered what the rush was. He wasn't exactly an A student, but he admired the ones that were. And he liked to watch her.

He saw her beautiful brown eyes, her long soft hair, and her curvy body. He always had a taste for good-looking women. He was the type of man that could see beauty in any woman. He was in love with how women looked, no matter the shape or size. And she was a natural beauty, but you could tell she didn't know it yet. He liked how innocent she looked. And he loved her style. She always wore a scarf, and he thought that was really cool.

Part One

She wanted to be loved and longed for all that came with love; that feeling of joy and the excitement of feeling beautiful—that new, fresh sensation of being with someone.

She was in love with the feeling she read in novels and saw in movies and she wanted someone to love her that way, but it seemed no one fulfilled her dreams.

She was lonely, so she found comfort in material things, like scarves. She had so many scarves. It probably meant nothing in the beginning—the habit of collecting scarves. But as the years and loneliness went on, the scarves grew; by the time she was thirty she had over 3,000 scarves.

Men were like the scarves she wrapped around her neck. In the beginning, she was in love with the scarf; loved the feeling of it on her skin. She could not imagine leaving the house without it. But by the end of their journey together, she was sick of the scarf. She did not even want to look at it. She often wondered where had the love gone? How could she love something so much one day, and then not even be able to look at it the next?

Well, not all the scarves were that way. There was always that one scarf.

Her favorite scarf was around her neck today. That would be her luckiest scarf of all her days to come.

She always knew when he was staring. **She would catch little stares and gazes, but today with that silky red scarf,** it seemed as though his eyes were always on her.

She had beautiful, olive-toned skin that did not need a lot of makeup, but like most women, she did not see it that way.

She felt comforted by the scarf around her neck, less exposed, less of a chance he would see her imperfections.

But if only she knew that he only saw beauty. And today was no different. He saw *her*. And at that moment, she felt beautiful because she could feel him admiring her.

Maybe it was the red scarf around her neck; maybe it was because their stars aligned at that moment. She wasn't sure. But she could still remember how he looked at her and she still got butterflies if she thought about it too long.

She wondered if they had been lovers in a different life, or if they were destined to be together. Although she was not the type of woman who held those thoughts dear—she did not understand fussing over a soulmate, she wasn't even sure she liked the word soulmate—but today, she was a believer. How else would she have such strong feelings for the guy across the room? She had never spoken to him— well she had, over and over, but only in her mind. But that would all change today.

The bell rang and she was a creature of habit, so she took a right and walked straight down the hall like she always did. Passing the cafeteria, she could see the shiny polished floors everyone walked through every day without much thought of who cleaned those floors the night before. She gave her usual humble smiles and bashful waves to friends and peers, some she knew well and some she knew not at all, but she was not rude. She walked like the true introvert she was and daydreamed through the halls with the fluorescent lights.

She started to wonder if she would ever get the courage to talk to him, John. He had such beautiful hazel eyes, one a little greener than the other. He had that rugged, but gorgeous look that made him look older than he was. He was sixteen perhaps, but he looked like a man—a sexy, gorgeous man.

She was not a flirt, and she did not usually let beauty stun her. She was not vain, but he was different. There was always something different about John.

She continued to daydream, thinking about one spring day when the birds would be chirping and the sun about to set. John and she would be snuggled under an oak tree, sharing the silence and beauty of nature.

Just then she felt a tug on her scarf. She heard his voice and froze. She could not even turn around. It was as if his touch—just a quick tap really—was filled with great power. She imagined what those magic hands could do if a simple tug was giving her goosebumps; if only she could turn around.

He said something again, but between the noise of the lockers, the smell of old pizza, the bright lights, and the chaos in her own mind, she could not make it out. Maybe she offended him that day, but that was not her intention.

She continued to walk on and headed straight for the exit doors. She could not get there fast enough. She was so embarrassed and felt so childish—why couldn't she just turn around?

Her heart was beating so fast and her palms were sweaty; she could feel John still behind her. She could feel his presence. He had that kind of ability; everyone knew when he was around.

He was fun-loving and popular, and she knew he had been with dozens of girls. She also knew she had not gotten past second base. What would he want with her? She had not even liked her first French kiss; it had been awful, and the thought of sex frightened her. He could have anyone; the disbelief was making her stuck and turning around was not an option.

Maybe he wanted to know what Mrs. Belsky said before the bell rang or maybe he was wondering what artist she was going to choose for the project due next week? Maybe he wanted her to go on a date, or maybe Homecoming?

No, no. She was not going to get ahead of herself; she always did that. Her mind would get the best of her. She just needed to get the courage to turn around.

By the time she got to the exit doors, he was making jokes with his buddies—she could hear the laughter. That was when reality hit her like a ton of bricks; she was about to get on the big yellow bus. The stale smell; the thought of so many others being there before her; that bumpy, loud ride home.

She tuned it out though and quickly found a seat. She looked out the little window to find him. There he was, walking across the parking lot, lighting his cigarette, high fiving his buddies, and winking at the girls. He was so cool.

It seemed like all the girls in his grade were beautiful, and it was well known which ones he had been with.

When she looked in the mirror, she did not see that beauty or have that confidence. She sat on that bus wondering what he had wanted to say? What would have happened if she had turned around? She so wished she could have been one of those confident, beautiful girls, but who was she kidding? She would have to be stuck with the what ifs.

When she got home, she was restless and wondered how she fucked it up so bad without ever even saying a word. Just then she got the boost of confidence she needed. Where was it a half hour ago? Never mind, she was going to act on it.

She was impulsive and determined to make it right. She knew he had football practice, so she threw her bag down and shut the front door. She headed back to school on foot.

As she walked down her long driveway, she thought about what she would say. She came up with dozens of excuses to talk to John if she got the chance. She would tell him why she hadn't turned around. And how she looked forward to her art class all week long. She would also tell him that meeting there once a week was hardly enough. She would tell him how Friday is her favorite day and 1:30 pm is her favorite time.

Then she would tell him that when she walked through Lincoln Hall, where all the juniors had their lockers, she always looked for him. She would let him know how he put a smile on her face the whole day if she sees him in the hall, in passing, and when he gives her a simple head nod hello.

Or maybe it was too late, she thought. He probably just thought she was a freak who could not even feel or hear, or maybe he thought she was stuck up and rude—but that wasn't her at all.

She thought of so many different scenarios on the five-mile walk back to school that she became frustrated, and by the time she saw the Pleasantville High School sign, she had forgotten all her excuses.

What did it matter? She probably would not have the guts to talk to him anyway. He was probably on his way to practice and she could not imagine he would give her the time of day after she ignored him.

As she turned the corner, there he was smoking a cigarette, standing by his 1988 Chrysler; he could make anything look cool.

She thought she heard something, but she froze—all those tight, tense feelings were back. But then she heard him call her name. She did not even know he knew her name. She never liked her name, but today was different. She liked the way it sounded coming out of his mouth.

"Julia, come here. I want to show you something," he said. She heard it loud and clear; there were no distractions this time. She loosened her scarf a bit, took a deep breath, and walked closer to the LeBaron. "I like that thing around your neck; it would look better on my floor though."

His eyes were so green in the daylight. She could just stare at them for hours. He smiled, and his dark long hair blew in the wind; there was an awkward pause. Normally, she would not take kindly to words like this, but she suddenly felt like she was right where she needed to be.

He laughed and said, "Lighten up, kid. I am just kidding. We hardly know each other, and I am a gentleman."

He was one of those charismatic people who could get away with saying anything. She said, "I know that; it was funny. What are you up to?"

He explained to her that the moon would be extra beautiful that night. It would be one of those rare moons, and he was not going to miss it. He asked her to get in his car and she was happy to oblige.

She opened the door, got in, and shut the door. He had Dire Straits playing, "Romeo and Juliet"—one of her favorites. She was so excited to be in his car, sitting on his passenger seat.

She could smell him; it was like nothing she had ever smelled before. He smelled like winter and summer all in one, which was fitting. John was light and carefree, but he was rough around the edges. He would always tell jokes, but she could tell he had a big heart underneath it all. And just maybe, someday, even a soft spot for her.

"Julia, did you hear me?" he asked. "I asked you if you were going to stay and watch the moon with me. It's hours away, but I am sure the time will fly by."

She had not heard him, but it was loud and clear this time around. She knew exactly where she wanted to be was right there in his car with all his attention. When she was with him, and it was just him and her, she could feel an energy that she would crave for years to come. Like a drug though, she would always want more, and it would never feel as good as this time. He lifted her up and made her feel beautiful in that moment. That kind of beauty was hard to find, and she knew she did not want to let it go right then and there.

But she knew she could not stay, not because she didn't want to, but because she had to be home. She had strict parents who would not be happy to know she was spending time with the handsome football jock two years her senior.

"I would love to stay, but I have to get home," she said. He looked disappointed, but only for a second. He never looked down for too long. Probably was too handsome to be sad, she thought. He could never understand her loneliness, nor would she want him to.

"Well, that's a bummer. Let me give you a ride home then," he said.

"No!" she said firmly, knowing her parents would kill her if they saw the LeBaron pull up their long, curvy driveway. "Thank you, but I will walk." She opened his door and stared at him for a second longer. She thanked him again and said goodbye. She could tell he wished she would have stayed, and she wished she could have too.

She walked home and was happy and sad at the same time. As she passed each stone walking up her driveway, she wondered what if he had brought her home? She imagined, what if he had kissed her goodbye? She was in the best daydream of her life when she saw her blue front door and realized she was back to her own reality. She would be stuck with the what if's—time to get back to what she knew.

She went to her room opened her drawer and gently took off her favorite red scarf. She folded it nicely giving it one last touch. She held it close to her face and she could still smell winter and summer, she could still hear his laugh and she knew she would long for more time alone with John.

But it was not the right time, she knew that, and he probably did too.

It wouldn't be until years later that they would meet again in that way.

She was twenty-two and she was enjoying life, as most twenty-somethings do.

She had learned to love all kinds of scarves, ones that had a practical purpose and kept her warm, and ones that were just for fun and fashion. The look was pretty much her trademark by now; she had a long-term relationship with these scarves. Some she really relied on and felt true comfort when she had them. She wore them around her neck, around her purse, in her hair, and she even had one hanging from her rearview mirror in her car.

She felt secure and safe with her scarves. And she felt incomplete if she did not have one of her many scarves with her—which was practically never. She had met a few different men at college and work, parties and bars. She enjoyed their time, but always felt like something was missing.

She thought of John now and again and when she did, she felt silly because she thought he would probably not even know who she was by now. He probably never thought of her again after that day in his car. She could remember everything about him, his smell and his smile, harvest moon, Dire Straits, and the feeling of his fingertips on her red scarf.

She even remembered how the moon looked on that September night in 1996, when she was in her room dreaming of John.

It had been a beautiful moon; he was right.

It was October 2004, and it was chilly outside. Her friends were having a Halloween party and she did not want to go. She had just been on a blind date the night before; her fourth one this month. She was drained and feeling a bit down and she thought a night in was calling her name.

She was a bit shy, and she was not in the mood to drink— which helped her feel less awkward and less, well, herself.

She liked to drink at parties because she could be whomever she wanted to be, and it wasn't Julia. Drinking alcohol gave her that freedom, but she did not want to put in all that effort and fake it, not tonight.

Tonight, she would stay in, so she told her friends she would just be curling up with a good book. She made herself the usual single life dinner that came in a frozen box, poured some orange juice, made some chamomile tea, and grabbed her favorite book, *All Creatures Great and Small*. But before she could even open the first page, she was distracted by the moon.

She looked out her window and looked up, as she often did, but tonight the moon would stun her. The beauty was overwhelming and undeniable. The moon was bright and full, it was that pink and orange color that was mesmerizing. She remembered the moon on that September night, eight years earlier, when she was only fourteen and he told her that he loved watching true beauty.

She was more confident these days compared to her teen years, but still struggled with relationships, trust, and knowing who she was. But at that moment she knew something was calling her, so she jumped in the shower and found her best outfit, brushed her long hair, and put on her lipstick. Then she hopped in her car and headed to the Halloween party.

When she found the house, she realized she had never been there before. She would be walking into a party unsure of where her friends would be.

Suddenly, feelings of fear and anxiety overcame her. She couldn't get out of her car. She was just about to change her mind and back out of the driveway when she saw a group of guys walking into the house. She could not have been more than twenty-five feet away, but she knew him anywhere.

She saw his hair was shorter, but his laugh was still contagious. The sight of him and the sound of his laugh were so comforting—instantly her fear and anxiety subsided.

She got out of her car and could smell the autumn night air as she noticed a fire pit out back. She wrapped her scarf around her neck and entered the party.

It was loud inside. The music was blaring, and everyone was dancing. She scanned the room quickly to try to find her friends, but it was overwhelming. She felt a bit discouraged when all of the sudden she felt those hands on her; it was unmistakable.

She turned around this time. "John!" she said happily, and he was just as pleased to see her.

"You changed your hair. You have highlights. They look good on you. You always were a hipster!" he said.

She could not believe what she was experiencing; she never thought he would remember her, and a hipster? Really? He thought she was cool?

She realized her hair had been highlighted for years, and said, "Yes, it has been years since we have seen each other. How are you?"

John said, "Better now." He smiled and she was hooked. She knew this was her chance. She let go and let loose. She danced and laughed; with a little help from Jack Daniels she was feeling like a whole new woman. The night flew by and she found herself around the fire pit with John's arm around her. He was playing with her hair and with the fringes on her scarf, and she prayed for time to stand still.

The sky was bright because of the beautiful moon and John said, "See, babe, this is what I wanted to show you many moons ago."

He remembered. She could not believe he remembered that day in '96. She laughed and played it off; she didn't want to talk about the past. She was right where she wanted to be, and she was looking ahead to the future. In that moment she could see them together forever.

The night was coming to an end; most people had already left the party. Not that it mattered to Julia, she only remembered seeing John—everyone else was a blur.

"Do you want to come home with me?" he asked her.

Of course, she did, but before she answered she thought about what her mom always said. She was reminded to play hard to get a bit because she wanted him to want her, but she didn't want to make it too easy for him to get her.

She said, "I would love to, but it's already so late and I have to work early." She didn't have to work early, but she had to say something.

"Alright," John said, "next time."

She leaned in to say, "Absolut..." But there he was so close to her face. She closed her eyes and just embraced the moment. The moment she always hoped for. The moment she dreamed of so many times.

His lips were soft, and he knew how to kiss. He was gentle and sweet and used just enough tongue. He gave her a little nibble on her bottom lip. He knew exactly what he was doing. His hands were on her waist and slid down a bit, and she liked it. His body was so close to hers—she could feel the warmth of him. He had smooth skin and hard arms. She almost gave into temptation.

She was just about to say, 'Let's go to your place,' when he pulled away and said, "Good night, darling. I hope to see you real soon."

The sooner the better, she thought. "Good night, John, and thank you for a wonderful night," she said.

He walked her to her car. She got in, gave one last wave, and pulled away. She turned on the radio and "Love" by John Lennon was on. She heard that song a million times before, but this time it meant so much more. She was so emotional, she almost cried. She was so happy she finally got to spend time with John. She had wanted him for so long. No reason to dream tonight; her dreams were already coming true.

John called her the next day. She was so happy that she yelled with joy when they got off the phone. Her cat looked at her like she was crazy. And maybe she was a bit crazy, after all, she was singing and dancing and completely high on life in that moment.

She was about to go on the date of her life. John asked her to go to the movies. She threw the rest of her pizza out and jumped in the shower. She got out her favorite lavender body wash and her favorite warm vanilla sugar lotion. She was careful with her makeup, making sure every eyelash looked right. She used all the brushes and tools she had to make herself look as pretty as possible. She was a natural beauty, but she just couldn't see it.

After her makeup was in place, she polished her toes. She chose a sparkling silver and matched her nails, too. She put her hair up in a ponytail and wrapped the red scarf around her neck. She hadn't worn it in years, and she was excited to have the red silk around her neck again. She picked out a fitting black dress and red heels that she had just purchased from DSW. She felt amazing. He was picking her up at 8:00 pm. It was 7:45 and she realized she might not be home tonight, so she fed the cat a little extra food, and gave him a little extra love. Then she was out the door.

He was just getting out of his car when she shut her front door. He said, "You ready to go? You look nice."

Nice? she thought. Well, she hoped she looked more than nice. But she brushed it off. Nothing was going to bring her down tonight. Maybe he was nervous too; maybe he didn't want to say beautiful, just yet. She started to get all caught up in her head, thinking about all the things that he had said, but she stopped herself. She was going to really try to be in the moment and enjoy herself.

They pulled up to the movie theater and he asked her what she wanted to see.

She said, "The Notebook?"

"Really?" he said. "I was thinking more Saw."

Horror movies were not her thing, but she thought maybe she could change—be open-minded for him.

He laughed and said, "I can tell that's not your thing. How about Napoleon Dynamite?"

She loved a good comedy. Her favorite movies were romantic comedies. She wasn't sure how romantic *Napoleon Dynamite* would be, but she knew it was supposed to be funny. "Perfect," she said.

In the dark theater, she could be whomever he wanted her to be. They sat next to one another in the middle row. She had popcorn—he had sour patch kids and soda. He offered her sips of the soda and candy and they shared the popcorn that was on her lap.

During the movie she felt sexy and courageous. Maybe it was the darkness and all the laughter, but she felt compelled to make a move. She was never an initiator, but he brought something out in her that she never felt before. She put the popcorn aside and went for his hand. He was happy to give it.

His hands were soft and clean, and they had this magnetic power over her. Soon they were snuggling and laughing at the silly jokes in the movie. She put her head on his chest; she could feel his heart beat. Probably not beating as fast as hers, she thought.

He kissed her on the head a couple of times, and it left her breathless. She didn't even remember the movie or the jokes that she had laughed at, but she remembered his soft lips gently kissing her forehead. She would never forget that.

After the movie, they walked out of the theater holding hands. He opened the car door for her, and she unlocked his door. He said, "What else do you want to get into tonight, darling?"

She thought, *You*. But she wouldn't dare say anything like that. She casually answered, "Whatever you want."

He said he should go let his dog out and asked if she would join him. She was happy to come along; she loved dogs. She loved all living creatures—especially dogs, they always had such a great spirit.

They pulled up to his house. She said, "So this is where you live? This is really nice."

Of course she knew where he lived. She'd passed it a thousand times before. Her best friend lived up the street and since they had been in fifth grade they would sneak peaks toward his window. She had had a crush on him, too, but then again, who didn't? It was said that even some teachers had had a thing for him. To Julia, John was the best-looking guy around; he won best looking in his sixth-grade superlatives, so she was not alone in this.

While all her friends were dreaming about Jordan and Joey from New Kids on the Block, and later Justin Timberlake from *NSYNC, she was completely mesmerized by John in fifth period art class. But she didn't want him to know that.

His parents gave him the house he grew up in. As an only child, he was close with his parents and they were proud of him. His mother must've known she had a golden child. They moved to Florida years ago, and he went down to visit often. His house was beautiful, and you could tell his parents still took care of it.

He brought her inside and a big, beautiful yellow Labrador came running over to him with happy kisses— and then smelled Julia.

She always smelled good. She was a classy girl who was genuinely kind; she never met a dog that didn't love her. Immediately, she fell in love with him; Toby was his name. He was harmonious; well mannered; had big, kind, soulful brown eyes; and a wet nose. She was happy to receive his kisses. She even loved the name Toby—one of her family dogs shared the name.

She knew once she entered his house she would never want to leave. They made their way to the living room and sat on the couch. It was comfy and had what looked like a hand-woven blanket over the back.

He poured two glasses of homemade red wine; he must have known that was her favorite. She looked around to see how he lived. Everything had a place, even Toby's toys. His house smelled like firewood and she realized he had an alluring fireplace. There were six pictures on the mantel of family and friends, and one of a dark brown dog—not Toby. She thought she remembered hearing he had lost his family dog in an accident, and he had been devastated. That made her sad, yet curious, but she did not bring it up.

She noticed there were no plants in his house and thought it would be a perfect gift for him next time she came over. She asked him to light a fire and they cuddled on the couch, even Toby was snuggling. It was perfect.

John said, "It's already past midnight; do you want to go home?"

She didn't want to go home now or ever. She imagined her life there, in his lovely home—Toby and her cat, Tigger, being best buddies. Toby and Tigger even sounded good together. Surely, they were meant to be buddies.

"No," she said. "I think I want to stay. If that's okay, of course." She could tell he liked that.

He scooped her up and whispered in her right ear, "It's more than okay." He kissed her ear with small gentle kisses, as he carried her up a few stairs to his bedroom. His bed was inviting with satin pillows and a down comforter. His room was warm, and it smelled like cherries. He must have lit a Yankee Candle while she was playing with Toby. He had Sade's *Greatest Hits* playing and it was the most romantic setting she could hope for.

They laid on the bed and started kissing; it was even better than the night before. His hands were all over her body. He took off her scarf, and he kissed all around her neck with little soft kisses that made the hairs on her neck and arms stand up. He gave her goosebumps and butterflies all at once. He took off her dress and rubbed his fingertips over her breasts softly and said, "You are so beautiful."

She could see it in his eyes; he liked what he saw, and he wanted more. He was gentle, but strong and confident. She followed his lead. She loved his body, too. His chest and arms were toned, his legs were long, and his back was muscular. He was everything she dreamed of and more. He made her feel things she never felt before and she didn't want him to stop. She moaned and said things she never said before. He liked it and tugged her ponytail back while kissing her neck and making her feel bliss— and he orgasmed too.

"You were made for me," he told her. "It fits perfectly, and I don't want to take it out." She felt it too.

"No Ordinary Love" was playing in the background, and the candle was still burning as he softly caressed her back and gave her little kisses on her neck. He counted her moles and studied her curves. He loved how soft her skin was and he told her that she had the most beautiful face he had ever seen. He took his long leg across her body and held her tight with his muscular arms. She felt safe and loved; something she longed for her whole life. They fell asleep in each other's arms. She fell fast asleep; the best sleep of her life.

A couple weeks later she was in Home Depot due to plumbing issues in her apartment. Her landlord never returned phone calls—unless you owed him money, then he was quick to pick up the call. Funny how money changes people, she thought.

She took a left out of aisle six and headed for the registers. She hated Home Depot. The store was so big, and it felt overwhelming to her. So many men everywhere; she wondered how women worked there. She thought they were so brave; she wouldn't have the guts to be the minority.

Just then she saw an adorable houseplant. She knew she had to buy it for John. Lately, she couldn't get him off her mind. It seemed like every other thought was about him. She made her purchases and headed home. When she pulled in her driveway she saw John was waiting for her.

"I heard you needed a plumber," he said. He had gotten her message. She had called and left him a voicemail. She had been complaining about her landlord but hadn't expected John to come help her.

She lit up; she was so grateful. She hugged him and said, "I have something for you." She reached into her car and gave him the plant. "It will brighten up any room in your house and clean the air." He loved how she was thinking of him, and he was grateful.

After they got everything in order, they spent the night in. John was exhausted after cleaning the apartment and she was happy to stay in. Her apartment was small and cozy, and she had a roommate that was never home. Her roommate was also her best friend since elementary school, and John knew her well. John's family and her family were close.

"Is Jackie home?" he asked.

"No, I don't think so. She's always with her boyfriend, and never comes home anymore." Julia wondered why he asked. Jackie was beautiful, actually, she was drop-dead gorgeous. Often when the girls were out, men would-be all-over Jackie. She had that classic pin-up look. She was blonde with big blue eyes, and her features were perfectly symmetrical. Her legs were long, her waist was small, and her breasts were full. She was a natural beauty for sure, but the best part of Jackie was that she was a genuine person.

She had a big heart and loved animals and nature. The girls had a lot in common and they bounced good ideas off each other. Jackie was an aspiring actress who was trying to write a screenplay. Julia had her degree in journalism, and she had about fifteen manuscripts under her belt. Some were finished, but she didn't love the ending. Some were only 10,000 words in, yet she wasn't sure what else to add.

Julia was always looking for inspiration and Jackie was always good for that, but lately, Julia was lucky if she saw Jackie once a week. Jackie met some guy in an acting class she took in NYC and apparently was head over heels in love.

With the apartment all theirs, they had an intimate night in—making love for most of the night.

They started a relationship and Julia felt extraordinary. It seemed as if anything John did he was good at, and his energy was rubbing off on her. They shared lots of love and laughs together. They sat outside in the summer on the deck and grilled burgers.

They played fetch with Toby, sat under the oak trees in his backyard, and watched the sunset. They drank wine and truly loved each other. They shared a passion that was undeniable, and she was so in love. He could not keep his hands off her, and she loved every touch.

He had this way about him—he was so confident—and it was contagious. She started to feel like she was someone special too. For the first time, Julia felt happy, at peace, and satisfied.

They took a few vacations together; they liked the same warm weather climates. Summer was their favorite season and Florida was their favorite state to visit. Florida was good to them; they loved how hot the air felt and how gorgeous the palm trees looked. Julia hoped one day they could move there. She always saw herself in Florida, writing books on her balcony overlooking the lavender fields, and hearing the ocean waves crashing on the shore—giving her the inspiration she needed.

The Sunshine State was always a dream away, but she thought anything was possible these days. After all, she was lying with the love of her life every night. She knew his parents loved where they lived in Coral Springs, Florida, so every once in a while she would drop hints to live there too. After all, she could work from anywhere; why not have a yard full of palm trees—instead of oak trees—and a beach you can use all year long?

For now, this was paradise. Sitting on the couch with him, playing cards, and watching documentaries with him, or having their friends over, and truly loving each other's company. They liked the same New York sports teams. In Connecticut, the fans were split between Boston and New York, and it was a big deal; could be a deal breaker. This was no problem for John and Julia. They had season tickets for the Yankees, and they enjoyed this together. They often went to the ball games with Jackie and her boyfriend, Tommy. Tommy was a little like John, and they got along well enough. He was attractive, pleasant, and funny. And you could tell he loved pleasing Jackie.

Jackie was always fun to be around, and she was easy on the eyes. John didn't seem to mind. Julia felt a little jealous in those moments.

They went out to dinner, went to parties, and liked the same music. He sang her favorite love song by Christopher Cross, "Sailing." He brought her flowers; they stayed in, and they ordered in. She cooked, did his laundry, and kept his house nice and neat for them. They went for walks with Toby, and they did just about everything couples do. After about three months she was pretty much moved in. She had more belongings at his place than hers. Even Tigger the cat made his way to 43 Summer Lane. Tigger and Toby became the best of friends, just as Julia hoped for.

John's birthday was in April and she thought they should go away to Florida for the weekend. His parents would be delighted to see her since they got along well. John decided it was a great idea and bought two tickets on the Jetblue website. He said, "Pack your bags, kid. We're going south; don't forget your bikini."

She was excited to get away with him for his birthday. He was turning twenty-five. He was at a good point in his life—with his career and his love life. His parents were proud, but they were always proud of him. He had the kind of mother who would do anything for her son, like most mothers, but she loved him dearly—you could see it in her eyes.

Julia never liked to fly, but when she did fly she preferred the window seat. Apparently, John liked the window seat as well. There they were in the aisle bickering over who would get the window seat. People were making her feel rushed, making comments such as, "Just sit down," while others were bumping into her. She saw passengers were trying to put their heavy, overstuffed suitcases above her in the overhead compartments, and she started to feel tense.

She just wanted to sit down, so she finally gave in and told John to, "Go ahead take the window seat." But she said it with a look that meant, 'No, don't take the window seat. Be a gentleman and give it to me.'

That was all he needed to hear. "Thanks, babe," he said, and brushed by her with a quick peck on the head. He sat down and put on his headphones. She sat next to him, in the middle seat with a stranger on her right. The stranger was harmless, but she would have preferred the window seat for so many reasons. She was a bit of a germaphobe, especially on public transportation. The stranger was using a handkerchief and she thought a handkerchief was the most disgusting thing in the world. She desperately wanted to offer the stranger tissues, but she figured that might be rude.

She looked to her left and John was singing softly, "Lucy In the Sky with Diamonds." His sunglasses were on, and he was bopping his head from side to side with a big bright smile. He had no care in the world. Must be nice to feel so carefree all the time, she thought. She felt a little bitter in that moment.

It wasn't all rainbows and butterflies. John seemed to get increasingly agitated by little things Julia would do. He wasn't too fond of Tigger either, which always bothered Julia, but she tried to ignore it. She hoped over time it would get better, but he was doing things that bothered her, too. She was trying to become a bestselling author and she wasn't having much luck with her manuscripts. Her latest project was about dolphins; they were her favorite sea mammal.

She was doing a lot of her research at Mystic Aquarium, which was about an hour away, and she wasn't getting paid to travel—these expenses were all out of pocket. But her pockets weren't very deep, and John often helped her out with the money she lacked. Even so, John wasn't supportive of her aspirations, so she began to lose faith in herself again. Julia was a 4.0 student when she was in college, she was a go-getter at her part-time job for the town newspaper, and just about everything she did, she put her whole heart and all her passion into. But she had insecurities that held her back, and by the seventh month, they were bickering, arguing, and becoming increasingly distant.

One night they had a big fight about money, and it left Julia in tears. Funny how money changes people, sometimes brings out the worst, she thought. She had just walked in from a long day of studying dolphins. Julia was tired and hungry. She didn't like to spend her money on food when she was out, and she forgot to grab a granola bar before she left this morning, so she only had a banana all day. She was "hangry".

She walked in the front door where she was greeted by Toby, who gave her many kisses like he always did. Tigger was rubbing on her leg and they both followed her to the kitchen cabinet where the treats were. Toby and Tigger both got so excited when Julia came home. They knew they were getting fed, plus she gave the best hugs and kisses.

She picked up Tigger and gave him a kiss, then placed him down where she put the cat treats on the floor. She kissed Toby and gave him a bone.

She talked to them like they could answer back, "Where is Daddy, guys?" She heard music coming from the other room. She walked through the living room and opened the door to the garage. There was John working on his motorcycle.

He loved to ride his motorcycle on summer days and nights. She took some rides with him, and even though she was a little scared, she trusted him. He also always listened when she told him to slow down.

"Hey, John," Julia said. He didn't move from the squat he was in. So, she went over to kiss him, and that's when he put his wrench down on the cement floor. It made a loud noise that startled her.

He stood tall and said, "You think I am made of money, don't you? You think you can take off all day and do whatever you want in Mystic, and I will put gas in your car and put food in your mouth? You are here all the time and you don't pay a dime, and that's fine. I don't want you to pay a dime. But then you complain you have no money all the time. Somehow though, you can afford to take these trips to Mystic to publish your..." he hesitated.

She could feel a pit in her stomach and knew he was going to put her book down—her baby, her love, her passion. He was never supportive. He always had to remind her she wasn't good enough. She knew he could have anyone, but she also knew she could too.

He looked at her, and she never saw his eyes look so cold. "...your stupid book." There it was, that one stung and it stuck too. Those words would haunt her for years to come; as if she needed another reason to not feel good enough. John didn't understand that. He was good at everything, but not Julia.

Julia knew failure and she knew what it was like to be the underdog and even the dog. Kids in third grade used to call her ugly, they made fun of her thick glasses, and they would say 'you're a dog'.

She looked at him with a tear running down her cheek. She could see he was filthy with motor oil all over his hands. She could see the dark circles under his eyes. She could see he was angry, but she knew this was more than the gas he put in her car yesterday. And he was right to an extent.

Maybe she needed to give him some money, but was this his way of asking her to move in with him? *Geez, don't be too romantic*, she thought.

She was hurt though, and she didn't want to say anything she would regret—she was mature that way—so she said, "I will go home tonight," and he didn't stop her. She said bye to Toby, scooped up Tigger, and went to her car. She thought for sure he would come out to stop her and tell her to stay, so she waited a minute or two in his driveway—it felt like an eternity.

He never came out to get her, so she pulled away crying.

She was sad when she left, but she wanted to make a point too. If he didn't want her there that was fine, but he didn't have to be so mean. She wasn't a leach; she was there because she felt welcomed. She wasn't trying to take advantage; she had her own bills. She had been paying for an apartment that she was hardly in, and by now it was just her. Tommy and Jackie had moved in together. They did it officially too—like Facebook official.

And that was another thing, he had a Facebook account, and he hardly had pictures of them as a couple. The ones he did have he only had because she tagged him in them. Julia brought this up before and he would say how he hardly goes on Facebook and he doesn't upload pictures of anything. And that was kind of true, but still, it bothered her a little—just a little.

She wasn't a big social media person either, but she was with the times, and that was just how it was—people put their personal lives all over the internet; like it or not, people will judge you accordingly.

She walked into her apartment. It was cold and the plants looked like they needed some serious TLC. She realized she hadn't been there in a week. She opened the fridge, but there wasn't much to eat, so she went upstairs to her bedroom. She laid on her bed and Tigger followed. She felt lucky to have Tigger—he always knew how to cheer her up. She snuggled him. He had a cute, pink, wet nose and little soft paws. His coat was fluffy and full—mostly orange with some black and white stripes.

She thought of all the things that bothered her about John, and she could feel her eyes fill up with tears. But then Tigger was playing with her scarf and scratched her neck playfully, quickly reminding her of better times. She got out of her funk, wiped her eyes, and remembered when they had been in Florida and danced all night. He had his hands all over her, and sexy people were dancing all around them. The reggae music was blaring, the drinks were flowing, and she was carefree. She thought more about the hot Florida air, and the sweat coming off their bodies and it was only turning her on more. She remembered how he felt close to her body. He was a good dancer; she followed his lead.

She remembered when they were on the beach and she had a little red bikini on. He rubbed suntan lotion on her back as he kissed her neck while whispering in her ear how sexy she looked in that two-piece. They laid in the sun until it set.

She longed for his arms around her once again. She closed her eyes, realizing she hadn't been alone in her bed in months, and it was kind of nice to be free. She fell asleep dreaming of better days with John—like it used to be.

One hot summer night, John came home later than normal. His schedule was usually regular, but lately, it was sporadic, and she could tell he wanted to spend less and less time with her. The little things he used to enjoy seemed to no longer give him pleasure. She knew it wasn't just her making him feel unsatisfied, but she wanted desperately to fix it. She was feeling pushed away by him, which made her want to grab on more. The thought of losing control of their relationship and losing him made her almost have a panic attack. She had loved him since she was young, she finally had him, and now she couldn't make him happy. It couldn't be.

She had dinner waiting for him, and even though she was starving, she waited for him to come home to eat. Bob Dylan was playing, "It Ain't Me Babe," one of his favorites. He walked in and she could just tell; she knew something wasn't right. The nights were getting colder and lonelier. She would have to be completely oblivious to not recognize their lack of passion lately. She wasn't ready to give up though. But she couldn't deny feeling it, and she couldn't contest how she couldn't make him laugh anymore. She missed that laugh, and she thought of ways to make him happy once again. Maybe they needed to get away; go to Florida—see his folks. Or maybe they needed time together—just the two of them—a romantic getaway.

She wasn't sure, but she knew she had to get him out of his shell. He was keeping to himself lately, more than usual. She got to understand him well over the months, but still, he was a complicated man. He was outgoing to all outside appearances, but he was a true introvert deep down, and he would not let anyone in easily. He had his own demons, she could tell.

He would stay up late in the other room, working on who knows what. Anything to not be in the same room as her. He was becoming irrational about the expectations he had of her. She was only working part-time at the newspaper; they were short shifts, and it was obvious Julia had other goals. Her main passion was writing, but he knew that when he met her, and now it seemed it wasn't enough. She worked hard trying to find someone to publish her manuscripts—and had some potential interests—but he thought it was time for her to grow up. He felt she should put her dreams aside, use her degree, and get a full-time job.

Julia was an independent woman and taking orders from a man—even John—was hard for her to swallow. They both were so stubborn and unforgiving that even little things turned into big issues. But no one would dare say the words 'break up'—not yet at least.

John was not happy lately—that was obvious—but he knew he had a good thing too. He knew Julia would do anything for him. She was perfect for him, even the plant she bought was perfect. It hardly ever needed water, which was good because he wasn't good about caring for plants. But the plant blossomed in the sunlight and gave the room color—she had been right. John knew since having Julia in his life, he had become a better person.

She brought out a soft spot in him that had a ripple effect on his family and friends. And they all adored her for it. Anyone could see the love she had for him. He had a supportive girlfriend and he was not ready to give that all up either, at least not yet.

It was a hot, August evening, dinner was cold, and she could tell John was too preoccupied to notice. Seemed like lately even when they were in the same room, he was a million miles away. She was determined to have a nice night though, like the ones they shared so many times before. So, she begged John after dinner to go for a walk with her and Toby.

"Please, come, John. I haven't seen you all day. It's a clear night; we can look at the moon together. It is supposed to be striking tonight," she said.

John thought about it for a second; she saw a shift in him. She thought she had him with the moon. He always loved the moon and all its beauty. "No, babe. I had a long day. We had so many calls today; I just want to watch the boob tube," he said. She hated when he called the television that.

John was a paramedic. He often came home tired and drained and just wanted to be left alone while he would unwind. She understood this, but there wasn't much time to play around with; even in the summer the sun set by 7:30 around there. She couldn't wait any longer to bring Toby for his walk, so she grabbed her linen scarf and Toby's red leash and headed out the door. She said bye to John, but it was as if she had already left—he hardly responded.

On the walk Julia felt so distracted in her own thoughts, trying to figure out how to make their relationship better, fun, light—like it used to be. She put her headphones on. She wanted to block out her thoughts, but not even "Hotel California" could help. She wondered if this was normal stuff couples went through and if they always bounced back. She really didn't know, after all this was her first real relationship. All the others were insignificant compared to this. She was so wrapped up in her thoughts that she wasn't even paying attention to where she was going. And just then Toby pulled her so hard, she tripped on the sidewalk. They never came to fix it—and she was usually so careful. The tree's roots had overgrown to the sidewalk; she had told them at the last town meeting, but no one cared, she thought.

"No, Toby! Come back, Toby!" she shouted. "Here, Boy! I have a cookie!! Where's Tigger? Toby Pleassse!!!" she begged.

Toby was a great dog, but he loved to run free. He followed his nose, like most Labs do. He wasn't a troublemaker, but she feared he would get into something unknowingly. She ran so fast trying to catch up to Toby, but she became so out of breath, she had to stop. She hung her head low and put her hands on her knees. When she looked up, she saw the red leash in the trees fading away. John lived near Sleeping Jumbo, which had traprock mountains and over thirty miles of land filled with trees and who knows what.

He disappeared so quickly into the trees, there was no way to know which way he went. She couldn't see Toby anymore, not even his red leash was in sight. She knew she had to go tell John; she got a quick burst of energy and she ran there. She passed the neighbors who were all friendly and waved her down. She could hear them asking where Toby went and if she needed help, but she just kept running. She knew John would know what was best.

She was frantic and emotional, and she knew this was going to be bad. She opened the front door, gasping for air. She looked around to find he was on the couch asleep with the TV blasting—some horror film. It figured, only he could fall fast asleep to the flashy sounds of a horror flick.

She ran to him. "John, wake up. Toby…" She had her head down, still out of breath. Her face was bright cherry red, and she ripped her scarf off and shouted, "Toby!" But she couldn't get the words out before he jumped up.

He loved that dog, more than he loved her, she thought at times—which she understood. Dogs are better than people. They are always happy and bring so much joy to you. "Julia, where is Toby? What did you do?" He was frantically looking around. His strong hands grabbed his soft black hair and he was pulling it while yelling. She couldn't even understand what he was saying. He was out of his mind, but so was she.

"John, we have to get in the car and go look for him," she said.

"No, I will go. You stay here in case he comes home. You already did enough damage." And with that, he slammed the door shut.

Julia felt awful. She opened the door and ran around the yard where she could see Toby's toys and bones. She longed to see his furry face. She called for him, "Toby, here, boy. Come home. Where are you?" she cried and pleaded. "Toby, please, come home." She felt helpless and guilty.

If she had been paying attention and not worrying about her darned relationship, and if she had been watching where she was going—enjoying the moment—Toby would be home safe. She didn't know what to do. She ran all around the neighborhood. She knocked on doors and asked the neighbors that were outside on this warm summer night, but no one had seen Toby.

Now it was after 7:00 pm. The sun was just about setting, and the moon was shining bright and starting to take over the night sky. Toby and John were both not home. Julia was pacing and looking out all the windows, calling Toby. Just then she felt warmness on her leg, it was Tigger. He knew something was wrong. She picked up Tigger and started to cry. She talked to him as if he could talk back, and she said, "Tigger, where could Toby be?" She placed her head on his soft fur and he rubbed his face against hers. It was comforting, but it also reminded her of Toby.

Her heart was racing, and it felt broken in pieces. *Where is Toby; where could he be?* she thought. Sleeping Jumbo had all kinds of animals roaming around. What if Toby came across a bobcat or a black bear? He would want to play; he didn't know any better. Toby thought everyone wanted to play with him. He thought everyone wanted to pet him. All he knew was love. What if he found his way to a fisher cat—she was always hearing about those on the news. Or a pack of coyotes. She and John could hear the coyotes howling most nights, and he was always telling her to keep Toby inside when they did.

She saw headlights pull into the driveway. She prayed for Toby to be in the passenger seat. She ran out to the driveway, but John looked disappointed. And she knew Toby was still missing.

She had never seen John look so sad. He opened his car door with his head down. He said nothing, just walked past Julia, as if she wasn't there. He opened the front door, walked inside, and shut the door. She knew that was it. Between all the fighting and bickering, and now this—it was truly over, she thought.

Somehow, she finally got a couple hours of sleep that night. She thought John stayed up all night. He was in the garage, working on who knows what, with his music blasting, and she knew better than to disturb him. They kept all the windows open and the garage door open all through the night, hoping Toby's nose would get him home safe and sound.

The next morning John got a call from the park ranger. Toby was found, unharmed, wandering in the woods. John leaped for joy when he hung up the phone. He didn't say anything to Julia, but she heard him cheer with joy and saw him jump in his car to go rescue his best friend.

When Toby got home, he was filthy and smelled like rotten eggs. Leaves were hanging from his fur and all four of his paws had a mix of mud and dried dirt on them. He looked like he got into something alright— probably happily running free, finally not on a leash, running in the streams. He loved to swim, she thought.

But he was happy to be home, she could tell. His big brown eyes were tired, and his tail would not stop wagging. Tigger walked over to greet his buddy and rubbed his face on Toby's front leg. Toby gave him a lick. Julia was thrilled to see him too. She didn't care what he looked or smelled like. She grabbed him and wrapped her arms around his neck, kissing his face. She wanted to know the details, so she jumped up, and asked John happily, "Where was he? Who found him? What happened?" But he didn't answer her; he didn't even look at her. He just walked past her like she wasn't even there.

She knew now for sure this was it, it was over for good. She wasn't even sure how it started—the arguing, the distance. She wasn't sure how to fix it. She just knew it was beyond repair.

Hard times would get the best of them and they could not get past some rough patches. Eventually they went their separate ways, after just one year together. It was mostly John pushing Julia away and she could not fight it anymore.

"This is the last of your stuff," John said. He handed her a box. "You don't want to forget this one; this is a special box," he said. It was raining outside, and her hands were cold and wet. She took the box and carelessly put it aside. She didn't care about her possessions at that moment; all she cared about was John. She just wanted to go back to happier times with him.

Julia went to embrace John. She was instantly warmed and felt safe in his strong arms. She hugged him tightly. They stayed as one for what felt like hours, neither wanting to let go. She couldn't even feel the rain on her anymore; she couldn't see or hear anything. She was nestled in his chest. She was numb inside though. This had really taken a toll on her. It was keeping her up at night. She wasn't performing as well at her newspaper job. And her book was on the back burner. She couldn't find joy in the things she used to. She couldn't get John out of her head for more than a minute.

She heard his heart beating quickly; she knew he didn't want this either. She knew he loved her, and he couldn't let go. She moved one of her hands to caress his cheek and she tried to speak, but she was speechless. There were no words, only tears filling her eyes. He kissed her a few times on her cheek, and once on her forehead. And he said with a broken voice, "You know, Julia, I will always love you." That was it; she was crying like a baby. She couldn't understand if the love was there, why couldn't they work it out?

She loved being his girlfriend. She loved being with him. She knew no one else would make her feel the way he did. She was overloaded with sadness. She didn't want this to end, and neither did he. She could feel it in his touch, his hands, his kiss. How did they get here? She practically begged him for another chance, but then he pulled away. She didn't even care at that point how she sounded or what she looked like, she was desperate. She pleaded with him and told him she would change. She swore she would get a full-time job. She would make him happy. She wanted another chance to make it right.

But he had already made up his mind, she could see it—now that they were face to face. His hands said one thing, but his eyes said another. Looking deep into his eyes, she knew it was over.

So, she turned away and left John and the box behind. She thought she heard him call to her, but she felt like she was fourteen again, and he was the cool football jock. Again, she wasn't good enough, but this time it was even worse. This time he had broken her heart.

She could feel her heart heavy, felt like it was shattered in pieces. Like when Toby was missing, but worse. She was not going to turn around this time. She kept walking in the rain. She knew deep down, somehow, that this would not be the last time she would see John, but she also knew, for now, it was over.

But John would remain in her life on and off for so many years to come. In fact, they both knew they could never truly be away from each other for too long. They both had some self-reflecting to do, but there was no denying their feelings. They had something true and special, and there was no denying that. No one touched her like he had.

He was right. She had a lot of growing up to do and five years flew by.

Now she was twenty-eight, and she knew who she was—at least she had a better idea. She published a couple of books, and she was working on promoting her dolphin project. She was proud of it. She knew it was something special because she knew people would be able to see the passion she had for it. People loved passion, and you couldn't fake that, she thought.

Eventually, she was awarded for her hard work. She finally had a best seller, *The Dolphin's Way*, she called it. Turns out all the hours of research were worth it. After John and she broke up, she devoted her time—too much of her time—to the project. Deep down she wanted to prove to everyone that she could be a professional writer. She wanted her parents, her friends, and of course, John, to be proud. She wanted John to see she was powerful, smart, and brave; just like him.

She also did it for herself. She was working on her self-esteem ever since John and her split, and she knew it was not an easy road, but she was determined. And when the book became a best seller, she was truly proud of herself. She hadn't accomplished anything like that since graduating UConn. She sent John a copy. He wasn't much of a reader, but she hoped he would read this one—after all, he was her muse.

She knew he still lived at 43 Summer Lane, but it had been a while since she was over there. Her car hadn't been parked in the driveway for some time. She missed the house and the oak trees; she missed grilling and playing cards with her best friend. She desperately missed Toby and she could tell Tigger did too.

One time she had been watching Animal Planet on the television, and there was a dog barking. Tigger had run over to the screen. She saw it in his big, yellow eyes; he missed his buddy Toby.

Most of all, she missed her love, John. He was irreplaceable, and she always knew that. Jackie always said, 'Don't be with a guy that you couldn't imagine being without,' and she never understood what that meant, until now.

But she wouldn't have wanted to have never been with John. Of course, breaking up was terrible and every day since had been so hard for her. Some days were harder than others. But she would not have wanted to miss the good times. The memories kept her alive and kept her believing. She always hoped their paths would cross again, like it had so many times before. She knew deep in her heart that she would be with him once again. Maybe they were soulmates, or whatever you wanted to call it, she thought.

She was more confident than ever before, but still, she longed for love. She would find herself staring at old pictures of her and John. She would read romance novels, wishing she could have just one more day, one more night, with John.

Their breakup was very hard for her and it would take maybe forever to get over him. The first few months after the breakup, she would call him on the lonely nights she spent with a bottle of Jack Daniels. He always answered. He would have her over, but morning would always come, and they would go their separate ways. He knew she would do anything for him, and he took advantage of that, she thought.

She spent so much time running back to him, but it never lasted because deep down she knew something was not right. Even John could not make her feel complete. She knew she had to make herself happy.

It was a cold, bitter day in February—February 14th, 2010, to be exact. She didn't like Valentine's Day, not just because she was single that year, but because she always disliked the Hallmark holiday. She thought it was silly to devote one day to celebrate the love in your life, and she thought every day should be treated that way.

Not to mention, when she was small—she couldn't remember exactly how old she had been, maybe five or six—her grandfather passed away right around the holiday. She remembered her mother being so sad. She was supposed to bring valentines to school that week, but her mother was in such a depression; she wasn't even coming out of her room those days. So, Julia went to school without any valentines. It wasn't a big deal. Her teachers were aware of the recent family passing, and they helped Julia make cards, but she always remembered feeling left out, sad, and lonely.

Her grandfather was kind, his house smelled like sugar cookies, and boy did he have a sweet tooth. He shared the sweetness and never let you leave his house without taking a bag of treats with you. Of course, the memories faded over the years, and the few Julia did manage to savor, she wasn't sure if they were true or something she fabricated over the years. She loved them anyway and thought of her grandpa often.

But it was 2010 now and all that had been buried for a long time. Her mother never discussed the details of grandpa's death, and Julia knew better than to ask. She never wanted to hurt her mom.

Julia was a bit tipsy that day, and she found her way to the local bar. She knew John frequented this place, and she was hoping he would be there that night. He never liked Valentine's Day much either; maybe he too would be drinking his sorrows away. She sat on the hard, uncomfortable bar stool for two hours waiting. She was feeling pretty good by now—she had about four Jacks on the rocks. She played the jukebox; she loved classic rock. She played "Tequila Sunrise" by the Eagles and "Chasing Pavements" by Adele; listened to "Riders on the Storm" by the Doors, and then "Here I Go Again" by Whitesnake, they understood her misery.

But when her songs were over the couple in the corner took the jukebox over. They changed up the genre with love songs. First Whitney, then George Michael, and then Lionel Richie. *Come on you two, go home, or get a room*, she thought.

She just wanted to forget all about love. She felt so lonely, and she just wanted to forget everything. She took her hand and gently rubbed her scarf, she felt a bit of comfort, and she started to think about when John would kiss her neck. She wanted to go back in time. She liked the way the satin felt on her fingertips and it reminded her how she missed his touch.

She wanted to see him, but she knew she couldn't call him tonight or drive over there and knock on his door, like she had so many times before. She felt like maybe it was time to go home, so she wouldn't do anything stupid. She could feel the Jack warming her body. She could feel her thoughts dissipating, and her hands going numb. She felt a bit out of control, like she couldn't tell right from wrong, and she knew in that moment she liked it. This was why she loved drinking. This was why one drink never felt like enough. She felt freed from herself, her insecurities, and her doubts.

But she was beginning to think Jack Daniels might get the best of her that night, and she didn't want to do anything irrational. She didn't want to wake up with regret on her mind.

So, she asked the bartender for the check. She knew her from school many years before, Trina. She was a nice girl, but they never were too close. They had a lot of the same friends though, and Jackie was one of them.

Everyone knew Jackie. Jackie's parents were at town meetings, they hosted parties, they knew everyone, and her whole family was very well liked. It was said one time that they had traveled to Italy and had run into over a dozen people they knew on the trip. They were popular, and so was Jackie.

Jackie never had the insecurities that Julia had. Julia was an only child and she felt her parents raised her right, for the most part. They gave her everything she wanted: art lessons, horseback riding, dancing lessons, but they also had such high expectations. They always pushed her. It was to the point where Julia always felt like they would never be satisfied with her accomplishments. Julia thought often that she could find a cure for cancer, and it would still not satisfy her mom and dad.

Her mother was a nurse and devoted her life caring for her patients, and her family. Her father was a lawyer, and Julia knew she could never argue her way out of anything with her dad.

Her parents wondered why Julia could not have a steady romantic relationship—they liked John. They enjoyed his humor. They respected his morals and his career choices.

They figured Julia must have messed it up somehow. But they gave her space with her personal life for the most part. They thought she would know what was best. But, they were not thrilled with her career choices. After all, they paid for four years at UConn and Julia wasn't really using her degree. Most times she was at work she was doing small tasks. Her dad didn't like how they would use her. She was like their go-fer he would say.

But her parents didn't understand her, and they never did. She was a free spirit and she loved her folks, but she was determined to make her own path. She wondered if she would have turned out different, better maybe if she had the support of parents like Jackie's. Her parents thought everything Jackie did was amazing. And it showed. Jackie was one of the strongest women Julia knew because of it. At least Jackie always knew her parents would have her back, and her self-esteem soared.

Trina handed Julia her tab; she only charged her for two Jacks on the rocks—she was good like that. Trina asked, "How is Jackie?"

Julia took out her wallet and looked at Trina. She was quick to answer and probably sounded a bit rude and jealous, but she didn't care—Jack Daniels helped her with that. "Who cares? Probably having the most romantic night ever with Tommy. He probably popped the question… whatever." Julia could tell Trina was a little taken aback. They all used to hang out when they were in seventh grade, and maybe even then—long before Jack Daniels had come into Julia's life—maybe she had been jealous then too. Maybe she was always a little jealous of her beautiful friend.

Julia was feeling down, and she was tired of watching the couple in the corner making out. She was tired of looking at the door to see if he would come through. And she was getting a little nauseous from the alcohol and the smell of popcorn. This bar did not serve food, but they had an old-fashioned popcorn machine that pumped out popcorn every half hour.

She knew she had been there too long when she heard the fifth bucket popping.

She slid her stool out from under her and put her feet on the floor. She wasn't really paying attention; she was too busy making sure she had the last drop in the rocks glass. When suddenly, she felt a draft. The door opened and she felt someone was looking at her.

She suddenly had a warm feeling come over her, and it wasn't the Jack. Even on this freezing night, with the wind chill, she knew that feeling well. She knew it was him. She turned around and there he was; he had just walked in solo. He was a sight for sore eyes, she thought.

He went right over to Julia as if he was meeting her there all along. "It's nice to see you here, gorgeous," he said. He always had a way of cheering her up. She instantly felt lighter and happier; safer and free. She could see in his eyes, he was happy to see her too. He took her hand; his hands still felt magical. He led her outside to the deck. No one was out there. It was way too cold tonight.

"Sailing," by Christopher Cross, was coming through the speaker, their favorite love song. And suddenly the sappy love songs that couple had been playing was fitting. He grabbed her close and he slid her scarf down just a little bit. He kissed her neck and placed the scarf back. He slid his lips down to the top of her shoulder—he knew she was ticklish there. She had instant goosebumps. He was so good with his hands and his lips; she was dazzled and hypnotized by his fingers, by his words, by him.

How did he always know just what to do? He had her so close; she could smell him. She missed that smell. She looked into his eyes as they kissed. They couldn't stop kissing. Their passion warmed her heart instantly. She knew this was right where she needed to be. He whispered in her ear, "I was hoping you would be here. I was looking for you tonight." He asked her to come home with him and she was happy to.

The next morning, she woke up to Toby licking her face. He was so happy to see her, and she had missed him too. She turned over to find John was gone. There was a note. It said, "I got called into work. Stay as long as you want. Thank you for last night." She was disappointed she wouldn't be able to see him in the morning light. She thought, was he really at work? She hadn't heard the phone ring. Did he just want to bail so he didn't have to answer any of her questions, like what did last night mean?

They had been down this road so many times before, and as much as Julia loved to be in his house on Summer Lane, she knew she didn't belong. She knew she wasn't completely welcomed. She knew this vicious cycle would never lead her to her happy ending. She wondered how they could share such passion between the sheets, but in the morning light, it was gone with the wind.

She got up. She felt comfortable there in his house. She brushed her teeth and was pleased to see that her toothbrush was still there. She opened the bathroom drawer and noticed some of her toiletries were untouched, this made her smile; maybe he was holding on too.

She put the kettle on to make some tea and took Toby out back. When she came in she heard the whistling of the kettle and fixed her tea. She sat down on the couch and looked around. There were now seven pictures on the mantel—one of John and Julia in Florida on the beach. Julia had a red bikini on. He loved that bikini, she thought. And he always loved that white scarf in her hair. John had his fishing rod in one hand. She remembered how peaceful that day was. John loved fishing, even if he didn't catch anything—she could see him relaxing with every hook to his bait.

She got up and held the picture frame in her hand and wondered why they weren't in Florida, next door to his parents, fishing, and watching baseball together. She imagined a life together that she knew would never happen, or at least not now. And in that moment she felt dejected.

She put the picture back to match the others, and she kissed Toby goodbye. Somehow she knew this would be the last time she walked out of John's house, at least for a long time. And it seemed Toby knew it, too. He gave her a few extra kisses and with that Julia was out the door. She looked back and saw the number 43 on the door, and she thought, that would have been a nice address—43 Summer Lane.

It was not until she was thirty-three years old that she found true love. The love she found she knew was forever. She knew it was not found in green eyes or funny jokes. She knew she could not find it in all the scarves she had purchased. She knew it was inside herself. She finally found peace within herself and loved herself. She truly understood what love was. It was true what everyone said: you cannot love anyone until you love yourself. And not one person can give you everything, it does not matter how great that someone is.

Love can only truly grow if you love yourself, and are willing to be open, and remain independent and free. She was more spiritual these days, which was opening her eyes. She was enjoying practicing yoga and meditating on a regular basis. She could feel the positivity working.

If only these lessons were learned when she had been younger. Maybe John would have loved her enough, if only she had loved herself enough. It had been at least two years since she had been with John. She knew how to reach him, but she didn't know if he would want her to. He hadn't reached out to her in some time. She wondered if he had a new lover, or maybe a few. She wondered if he ever thought about her, and if he did, if he missed her. She would dream about him and his hands—that magic touch. She longed to see him, but she could not bring herself to call him. She just felt it wasn't right.

She was driving home from the farmers market she liked to frequent in Western Haven. It was a little after 4:00 pm. She could see the sun starting to come down through the trees. The air was cool, and she had her window opened slightly. She was daydreaming when John Lennon's song "Love" came on the radio. And it got her reminiscing about that Halloween night in '04. She looked in the rear-view mirror. She had more wrinkles on her face and neck these days. She fixed her scarf to hide the deepest wrinkle in the center of her neck; she hated that wrinkle. No matter how much she loved herself, she still thought it was impossible to love that ugly wrinkle across her neck.

She brushed her bangs to the side with her fingers to try and hide the few grey hairs she grew to hate, as well. They were so stubborn. She plucked them and they would come right back. Why is it that way? The things you don't want always come back to you, and the things you long for stay away?

Just as she looked back through the windshield she realized the light was red, but she was too far passed to stop now. She braced herself and kept driving. She closed her eyes, put her right foot on the gas, and went for it. She always remembered what her dad said, most people get into an accident because they hesitated.

Bammmmmmm. The loudest crushing sound she had ever heard, and she was out.

She heard sirens. She was shivering, and she felt like her head was spinning. She remembered she wanted a blanket or her scarf; she was trying to reach for her scarf around her neck. She was sure it was there, but she felt paralyzed. She couldn't move her arms no matter how hard she tried. She could hardly open her eyes. She could hear noises, like people yelling to her, but they were so far away she couldn't make out what they were saying.

She could smell meat and smoke. She could hear metal screeching and she knew something terrible had just happened.

"Can you hear me?" She made it out. "Yes," she was trying to say. She was trying to nod her head, but she couldn't do that either. Her lips felt sealed shut; she wasn't sure what was going on. And all of the sudden, she could feel the hot pavement and now she could smell rubber burning.

She thought this was it, and her life started to flash before her eyes. She remembered when she was a child and she was outside playing with her dogs. The neighborhood kids would come over and play. She remembered she had a treehouse they would play in. She remembered when she fell out of the tree house and broke her arm. This felt much worse, she thought.

Suddenly, she felt warm, strong hands on her; she knew those hands anywhere. "John," she couldn't say his name, but she tried. Her lips moved a bit and her eyes swelled a lot—the tears pouring down her face.

He wiped them away and whispered in her ear, "I'm here, babe. I have your red scarf. It's always in my pocket. I am going to wrap it around you now. You are strong. You are safe and I love you. There's a box of thirty scarves that you left behind. I saved them for you all this time. You stay strong so I can give them to you." She remembered trying to smile, then she remembered hearing helicopters, and then she remembered nothing.

In the hospital room, she remembered feeling cold and confused. She remembered there was a team of doctors around her bed and at some point they had a machine monitor they were all looking at. It had red marks that looked like fluid moving up and down, she didn't know what all the fuss was about, but everyone was in a panicky state.

She couldn't feel her legs and she couldn't hear clearly. Her eyesight was poor, but eventually she was able to make out that she was bleeding internally. The nurses rushed her away on the bed. As she laid flat she could see the white walls flashing by and she could still see the bright lights gleaming down if she thought about it too long. She heard someone say count backwards with me, 10... 9... 8... Then she saw black.

She woke up in an MRI; she hated enclosed spaces. She was trying to talk. She wanted some water. She was having trouble moving her lips. They must have seen her trying because she heard them say, "Julia, stay still. We will have you out of here shortly. We are screening you, and everything is looking good, but please try not to move for a little longer."

She was so confused and so cold. She just wanted to feel some warmth. She wanted her scarves. She wanted her Tigger. She wanted John. Did she dream of seeing him? She thought it must've been a dream.

Part Two: John

He saw her every day; he looked for her. He enjoyed watching her curves. She had a beautiful smile and a humble giggle that made him laugh back. He was inspired by her talent in art class and he knew she was a good student, something he was not, but what he lacked in grades he made up for in just about everything else he did.

He was a good football player, he had tons of friends, and parents that loved him. He thought it was sexy how smart she was. He mostly got Cs and sometimes Ds, but he flirted his way out of a few Fs. He was handsome and charming, and he never had to worry about finding a date. All the girls wanted to date him, even one of his teachers would get a little too flirtatious with him now and then. He did not mind though, he loved the attention. He was funny and confident, but he was kind, and he loved most animals, especially dogs.

It was September 1996 and he had just been told he wasn't able to play in the football game tonight. He was in trouble because of a detention he received earlier that week for smoking a cigarette on school property. He thought this was a ridiculous punishment.

He was standing at his car, talking to his buddies, when the principal saw him and asked him to put the cigarette out, but John refused saying he was just about to leave. The principal was not happy with him and for that, he served an after-school detention.

His coaches didn't want to bench him, but they had no choice. He knew he wasn't going to practice after school.

If they weren't going to play him, he wasn't going to show up.

Last period on Friday was art class, and he enjoyed it, not because he was artistic, he just needed to fill his schedule up and he figured art would have some pretty girls, and he was right.

He was always attracted to her; she was a natural beauty. She had curves at just fourteen, and he didn't know much about her, but he was curious to find out more. He wasn't sure what he was going to say to her, but he would think of something—he never had a problem talking to girls. The bell rang and he followed her out of art class. He could smell her; she must have just put lotion on her hands. As she walked away he could smell hints of vanilla. He liked vanilla, so he decided to tell her how pretty she looked today in that red scarf.

He tapped her on the neck softly—he was intrigued by the scarf. No one in high school wore scarves like she did. He was surprised when she didn't turn around, so he touched her again. She was soft and warm, and he wanted her to turn around. He always thought she had the most beautiful face; she didn't need a lot of makeup. She had such an even, glowing skin tone, he thought.

By the time he passed the cafeteria, his teammates were calling his name. They came over and walked outside school beside him. They asked him why he wasn't going to practice, and he said, "Coach can kiss my butt. I'm not going to show up now just so I could sit on the bench later." His buddies laughed and high fived him and as they parted ways he realized the cute girl from art class was gone, so he walked towards his car. He passed some of the girls in his grade; he was sick of the way they acted, not all of them, but a lot of them threw themselves at him, and he wasn't complaining, but he longed for something more.

He thought a girl that would play hard to get would be a lot more interesting, and he was always up for a challenge. He hung around the parking lot and smoked his cigarettes with a couple different cliques. He didn't care if the principal saw him; he wasn't doing anything wrong. The principal was always picking on him. But John didn't care.

Maybe because Mr. Johnson was friends with John's father, so John always knew he couldn't get into that much trouble. Plus, he didn't mind detention, the teacher was good looking, and he always had friends that were there or that he made easily.

Detention was a breeze and he wasn't going to let anyone tell him what to do. Anyway, he was kind of happy to skip practice after school that day. It was a beautiful day to be free. And the game tonight, well, he could think of a thousand things he would rather do, or at least a few. Practices were getting to him. He was exhausted in the morning, and not that he ever liked school all that much, but it was becoming harder for him to wake up and go.

He could use a break and now he was able to do whatever he wanted—he felt like he could get into anything. He heard one of his classmates talking about the moon tonight in his fourth period science class, and he always loved the moon. Harvest moon, I think she called it, he thought.
So, he decided he would linger a bit, and see if anyone wanted to catch a glimpse of the moon with him tonight. He talked to some friends, and one by one everyone left.

So, he walked over to his car—the piece of crap his parents gave him when he got his permit, but whatever, it was good enough. It got him where he needed to go.

He was finishing his cigarette when he saw her turning the corner. She looked so innocent and beautiful. She still had that red scarf on. He called to her. She got into his car and he liked the way she smelled. He could smell even stronger hints of velvet French vanilla, and it warmed him. He liked the way her face looked in the daylight.

The sun was hitting her brown eyes, just enough, and when the sun went in the clouds he could still see them shine; he couldn't find any imperfections on her. She had some moles on her arms and a few on her face and he wondered how many moles she had in total, and where they were on her body. He thought maybe someday he would be lucky enough to count them. He was surprised when he asked her to stay with him and watch the moon—she declined. He didn't know what he had done wrong. She was sending him mixed signals, and he was curious, but he wasn't going to chase her. He never chased anyone. He liked how she wasn't easy though. The last girl that sat in his car was quick to take off her clothes.

Julia wasn't like that, and he liked the freshness of it all. She was like a fresh breath of vanilla potpourri, he thought.

But before he knew it she was out of his car, and out of his life. He always remembered how bright her eyes were, her vanilla scents, and how gorgeous her smile was.

It was Halloween 2004, and he was on his way to a party in Newest Haven. His buddies were picking him up and he was happy to get out of the house. He wasn't going out much these days; he was spending his nights studying for his tests.

He was going to be a paramedic, like his father. He knew that was what he always wanted to be, and he was done goofing off. He knew he had to find a career he could see himself in for the rest of his life.

He pictured a beautiful wife and lots of dogs when he thought of his future, but he was single for now. No girls were going to distract him from his dreams, no matter how pretty. He was determined to pass and save lives.

He was never a good test taker, not because he wasn't smart. There were plenty of things he was good at, but he always felt distracted when it was time to get the number two pencil out.

But tonight, he would be celebrating passing all his written exams to become a paramedic, and he was excited to let loose and be carefree once again. He left his house in his favorite white t-shirt, brand new Timberland boots, and a dark pair of jeans that showed off his nice Bruce Springsteen butt.

He had been compared to Bruce before, and John Stamos a few times. That was fine with him; he always loved rock and roll. He could see himself in a band; he would love the attention. But he didn't have any musical talent. He wasn't too sad about it; he had plenty of other talents.

His friends picked him up at 9:00 pm. He was happy to see the headlights pull in. He gave Toby an extra bone and a pat on the back and told him to be a good boy.

"You finally coming out tonight, dude? It's about time. It's good to see you," said Joe happily. He and Joe had been friends since they were young.

Joe and John were inseparable from a very young age. On the playground, in elementary school, they held the record in kickball. They both loved kickball, dodge ball, baseball, anything with a ball.

They were rough. They were jocks. They were boys, and Joe was happy to see his old pal. Tony was in the back seat. John met Tony in high school. An Italian kid with a little attitude, but he was loveable. He would have nicknames for everyone.

"Hey, Johnny Boy! Where you been hiding? It's time to go out with your boys tonight. Let's get you laid." Tony was obnoxious and loud. He was short, but what he lacked in height he made up for in looks. He was just as charming as John; his features were handsome and even though he said what was on his mind, he had a way of making it funny. Tony had many talents and one of them was making you feel like you were the only one that mattered when he talked to you.

They were picking up Ziggy, their old buddy who lived down the street. Tony called him Marley because he loved to smoke weed.

Ziggy got in and they were on their way to the party. Marley lit up a joint, true to form. He took a puff and passed it to Joe. Joe liked to smoke every now and then.

He was a construction worker, and smoking helped calm his muscles and relax. Joe passed it around and turned up the tunes. Thin Lizzy's "The Boys Are Back in Town" was on, and they all sang along.

When the joint came to John, he said, "No, no. Not tonight, guys."

"Oh, come on," Joe said. "What's gotten into you lately?"

Tony shouted, "Pussy."

John didn't talk like that and he didn't like being called that either. Sometimes Tony annoyed John so much, and it wasn't just because it seemed like whatever girls slept with John, slept with Tony. But he knew there was an unspoken competition. He turned around and looked at Tony and said, "Calm down. I gotta take a piss test tomorrow. When I pass, we can celebrate."

And that was that. They were off to the party. John was happy to be with his boys. He walked into the party laughing. He had to admit it; Tony was funny. He wondered if she would be there. He thought about Julia every now and again, and when he did, he felt silly because he didn't really know her all that well. But that day in his car… the smell of musky vanilla. It always reminded him of her.

He went to get a beer from the keg outside. He saw the fire pit out back; he thought it would be nice to sit around it later. For now, he would go inside and see if he could find Julia or at least a good version of her, he thought.

He had some foam on his fingers from the beer overflowing, so he licked it off his fingertips, and just then he felt a draft. The door opened; there she was. He had a feeling she would be there. He was so glad he came out tonight. He made his way over to her through the crowd and said, "Hey pretty lady, nice to see you. Remember me?"

Julia looked fun and full of life. He missed her bold brown eyes—he was happy to see her again. They made their way to the fire pit. He introduced her to some of his buddies—most she knew or at least knew of. It was a small town, South Haven, population just under 10,000.

Tony kept telling John to seal the deal tonight. He was even more obnoxious when he drank. John usually wasn't so forward, but he was so happy to reconnect with Julia, so he just went with it. He asked her to come over. He knew it was late, but he didn't mind. He didn't even care if they stayed up and watched movies for the rest of the night, or if they just snuggled, or if they kept it completely PG.

He just knew he wanted to be near her. But Julia had to go. He was disappointed, but before she left he knew he wanted to see her again. Like tomorrow, well later that day—it was already the wee hours of the morning. "Can I have your number, so I can call you tomorrow... today... You know what I mean." He pointed up toward the sky; it was getting brighter by the minute, and the birds were starting to chirp. "Of course, I would like that," she said.

She was well mannered and polite and always smiled when she spoke. She reached for her purse, it had a blue scarf around it. She grabbed a purple pen and wrote down her number with a heart after the initial J.

He was happy to get her number, he had wanted to call her for years, and now he finally had her digits. He was interested in how her mind worked, and he wanted to know more. She looked like she was always thinking, like ideas were all around her. And her style turned him on. He loved her scarves, it kept this mystery about her, and he was hooked.

She was inspiring to him and he liked how artsy she was, even the way she signed her name with just a cursive J. He had never been around a girl quite so interesting as Julia. He always felt there was just something about her. She drove away and he looked at her number one last time. He smelled the paper; there were hints of vanilla. He liked the way it smelled. He folded it up in fours and put it in his pocket. He knew he wanted more.

He woke up with Julia on his mind, and he knew he had to see her. He had first shift today at his new job, and he was a bit nervous. But he knew the guys. He was also a volunteer firefighter for years now, so he knew he would be okay. He would be out by 4:00 pm and he would call Julia then. He went to work early; he was always on time. He told some of his buddies at work about Julia; they could tell he was happy to talk about her. His eyes lit up when he said her name—something they'd never seen in him before.

One of his co-workers was also one of his best friends; he was a good guy. All the guys John hung out with were good, but he and Brian had a special bond. They had a lot in common. They worked in other places together, too, before this job—like at the local gym. "You gonna call her tonight, bro?" Brian asked.

John nodded. "What should I ask her to do? Dinner? Bowling? What if there's nothing to talk about? You know I am not much of a talker."

"Well," Brian said, "just go to the movies. You like the movies; she probably likes the movies, too. Everyone likes the movies. And that way you won't have to worry about too much conversation." Brian always had John's back. They were good for each other, in their personal lives and on the job. John felt relieved. Brian always knew what to do.

He came home about 4:30 pm and put his feet up for a while. He liked to veg out after work and hang with his dog, Toby. Toby loved to snuggle on the couch with him; they were a good pair. He took a nap and woke up later than he had wanted to. He realized it was past dinner time, so he decided he should call Julia before it got too late. He was a little nervous. His palms were a bit sweaty, but maybe that was from the fire. He had a nice fire going, he always had firewood in the house. He loved warming his house this way. His fireplace was big, and you could tell he spent a lot of time using it.

On the mantel, there was a picture of a chocolate Lab. He loved that lab; his name was Bo. Bo was just about the best dog anyone could ask for and John and Bo were inseparable since John was five years old. They did everything together; Bo slept with John every night at his feet, faithfully. One day, Bo got loose, he ran to the street, and before John could save him, got hit by a UPS truck. John picked him up off the road and cried all the way home with Bo in his arms. He was only eleven years old and he would never be the same after that.

He got up to put the coffee pot on; he loved coffee—it kept him going. He enjoyed at least five cups a day. He took the paper out of his pocket, unfolded it four times, and there it was, J with a heart. He put the paper to his nose, and he could smell her—the warmest vanilla he had ever smelled.

He dialed the numbers then smiled when he hung up. He was picking her up at eight, and he was never late. He got there right on time, just as she was walking out her front door. He saw her hips in this black tight dress. He saw her legs shining even in the evening light. Her spotlight turned on, and he said, "You ready to go, gorgeous?" He would never forget the way her scarf looked that evening, with her hair in a ponytail, bouncing gently as she walked. He knew then and there he was not going to be able to keep his hands off her. He remembered Brian told him *Napoleon Dynamite* would be a good choice, it was supposed to be funny, so he suggested it. "Want to see Napoleon Dynamite?" She was happy to oblige. Julia was agreeable and sweet; you could tell she wasn't confrontational—and he liked that.

He loved sour patch kids; those were his favorite. So after he bought the tickets he knew he would be headed right for the candy line. He asked her, "Do you want a soda, or popcorn, or anything, doll?"

She answered, "Popcorn, please." And he saw her reach for her purse. She had a little purse that was hanging by a long strap, it was black, and it had a silver scarf wrapped around it, hanging over the flap. He noticed it matched her nails. She always had good style, he thought.

He could remember when he was in high school and he would walk past her; she would put a smile on his face all day. He always thought she was beautiful, graceful, and unique. And that face; she looked like Jessica Alba and Cindy Crawford mixed together—two of his favorites. She was simpler though, at least all the other times he had seen her. But tonight, he saw her in a whole new light, and he was blinded. She was so sexy. She had these red heels on; they looked brand new and they shaped her calves. He couldn't help himself. He had to stare.

She turned to him and said, "Here, take this." It was a ten-dollar bill.

"No, thank you. I got it," he said. He paid for popcorn, soda, and of course his sour patch kids. They sat in the middle row and he was happy they chose a comedy. He was a horror movie fan, but he didn't mind a laugh or two either. It was a silly movie, but they snuggled, and he loved to hear her laugh. Julia had a contagious laugh, and she looked even more beautiful when she was happy.

John loved spending time with her. He was seeing her regularly, and he was enjoying the ride. One day he got a voicemail from her, she sounded upset. Her landlord wasn't returning her calls. Her toilet was overflowing. He was no plumber, but he was good with his hands. He drove over to her apartment after work. He knew where Julia lived, he had passed it a few times. She lived with his parents' friend's daughter, Jackie. He always thought she was pretty, but she was a little stuck up for his taste.

He pulled into her driveway. It was a nice little neighborhood, about ten minutes from his house. There was a lake near the house, so he got out of the car—he always loved nature. He smelled the musty, earthy odors in the air; he saw a frog. He watched the frog's back legs jump to the lily pad, and he smiled because the frog felt safe there. He did too. He looked up through the trees to the blue sky. He always liked fall. The leaves changing colors always reminded him of true beauty.

In Connecticut, he felt he was lucky to experience all four seasons—the change was breathtaking. He looked to the right. There were several hydrangeas and all different colored mums in the yard. He thought it would be nice to bring her flowers the next time he came by. Julia pulled up in her 2002 green Honda; it was a light mint green color with a shift stick. He thought it was cute that she drove a 5-speed. Most girls he knew didn't know how to drive standard.

He said, "I heard you could use a plumber." He could tell she was happy to see him. She reached for something through her passenger window.

"I bought this for you," she said. He was taken aback. No one ever really bought him anything—well only his mom. She would send packages up from Florida. She never missed a holiday or a birthday. She even sent things just because.

"Thank you," he said, but he thought, *Oh man, I am really not good at taking care of plants.* "I hope I remember to water it," he said, half-jokingly.

Julia said with a smile, "Don't worry, you don't have to give it water too often. I think like once a month it needs an ice cube, easy peasy." She always had all the answers. She was smart, and he liked that about her.

After he cleaned up the mess, he cleaned himself up and figured they should have a nice night in. "Is Jackie here?" he asked.

"No," she said. *Perfect*, he thought, a nice quiet night in, just the two of them. He loved when he was alone with her. She cooked a nice meal. He remembered the way the butter melted on the bread. She had it spread perfectly— he enjoyed simple things like that. Whenever he made toast he could never get the butter to spread evenly. He was always too rough, and the bread would end up with a hole. But she made these delicious rolls that he could dip in the sauce and eat with his pasta that she made so nicely.

She had dark yoga pants on; he liked the way her butt looked in them. Her sports bra was blue, he could see it through the t-shirt she had on, and he asked, "Did you go to the gym earlier?" Julia worked out often, you could tell. Her body was toned, but not too toned—she still had curves. He loved her curves.

"Yes, I have to go take a shower. Do you mind?"

Do I mind? he thought. 'No way. Can I come?' he wanted to ask her, but he wouldn't dare, not yet anyway. He liked when things happened organically. "Of course not. Take your time," he said. She set him up with his feet resting on an ottoman. Gave him a beer and put the TV on.

"I'll be right out," she said. He flipped through the channels on the boob tube. He could smell the candle she must have lit before she got into the shower. *Smells girly*, he thought, and suddenly, he heard a thump. He was distracted by her cat.

Tigger, he thought he remembered was his name. He was orange, white, and black. John wasn't a big cat person.

He would never do anything to hurt Tigger, but he didn't want Tigger too close to him either.

Tigger was now on the ottoman, right by his left foot. He looked like he was studying John. John never had a cat before. Sure he'd been around a few, here and there, but he didn't go out of his way to get close to one. *But this cat, what did it want, and why is he just staring?* John thought. He understood dogs. Dogs were transparent. You knew what a dog wanted when he looked at you, and when a dog's tail wagged, it was a good thing. Why was his orange tail wagging ever so slowly? And his eyes were oh so big and yellow. He was pretty sure they hadn't blinked in a while. Why was he studying him? *Should I take his feet off the ottoman?* John thought. But he didn't move. John studied Tigger back.

"Hey, you." Julia was back. *Lifesaver*, he thought. He was afraid Tigger was gonna take him out. He looked up; she was standing over him. She had a cream-colored satin robe on. She had nothing on underneath. He could see her nipples showing. Her long brown hair was still wet from her shower—he felt a few drops. He completely forgot about Tigger and everything else. He knew this was exactly where he needed to be. She took his hand and brought him to her bedroom. He followed her lead. He could smell the rose scents coming from the candle. Chopin was playing, he was warmed with romance. She took off her robe and laid on the bed. He loved her body. He couldn't imagine ever getting sick of it, and in that moment he imagined them together forever.

They were spending so many days and nights together, and he enjoyed having her at his house. They hardly ever went to her place; he had to be home for Toby. He could still remember the day she begged if Tigger could come over when she was there, which was all the time.

He wasn't sure if he was ready for all this. He was the kind of guy who liked his freedom and his space, and he didn't mind sharing it with her, but Tigger. He wasn't scared of him or anything, obviously, he could take Tigger if he had too, but he didn't trust his yellow eyes.

He loved Julia and when she pleaded, "John, I miss Tigger so much. I want to be here with you, and when I go home every day for him, it's silly because I just want to be right back here with you. I feel more at home here lately than I do at my apartment. I just miss Tigger. Please, can he come stay for a bit?"

He could see it in her eyes, she missed her cat and he didn't want to see her sad. So, he said, "Okay, we can try it out. We have to make sure Toby doesn't mind. But if they can get along, he can come here when you are here." Which is all the time, he thought. She threw her arms and her legs around him; she was thrilled, and he was happy because she was happy. Tigger and Toby became the best of friends, and he wasn't that bad after all. Tigger was lazy, and he didn't need much from John, so it wasn't too much of a problem. But John had to get used to the whole litter box thing, and he thought a litter box was the most disgusting thing in the world. He wasn't a germaphobe, but come on, the litter box stunk.

It wasn't just the smell of Tigger bothering John lately. He had always been a first responder. When he was fifteen, he became a certified lifeguard through the American Red Cross. When he was eighteen, he became a volunteer firefighter. He was used to being in emergency situations. He always wanted to save lives, ever since he was eleven years old. He could never forget why.

It was 1990, he just got home from school; his parents were still at work. His mom was a high school English teacher and a swimming coach, so when she had practice after school she would have the neighbor come over and watch John for a couple of hours. But John didn't see his neighbor when he got home that day, and he knew Bo needed to go outside, so he decided he would take Bo for a walk. He grabbed Bo's blue leash, and he opened his front door. He thought he hooked the leash on Bo's choke collar. He heard it click. Bo had to be leashed; he was a runner. He was a great dog, but he hated the leash, he never learned to heel when the family took him for walks.

John freaked, he still had the blue leash in his hand, but Bo took off running. John threw the leash down, left the door wide open, and took off on foot. John ran as fast as he could. He was fast, but Bo was faster. "Bo, come back, boy. Please, Bo," John begged. Just then, a big loud truck appeared. John saw it from afar. Bo always barked at big trucks, especially UPS trucks. No one ever knew why, but Bo got so rowdy when the UPS guy would pull up to 43 Summer Lane.

"Nooooo," John cried, screamed, and pleaded. "Stop! Please, my dog!" There was nothing anyone could do. Bo met his fate. It was awful, and John would have to scoop up his best friend and take him home with tears pouring down his face. The neighbors were outside waving him down, calling out his name wanting to help. John remembered hearing sirens, but it was too late. That would be the worst day of John's short life, and it left him jaded for years to come. Today he was a man, but when he looked back to when he was eleven, he can still remember the heartache, the pain, the pit in his stomach. He knew he would never truly get over his best buddy, Bo. But since then he hadn't lost a love; his family was blessed that way.

Work was taking a toll though. It seemed like overdoses (ODs) were every other call these days. He worked in Western Haven, a few towns over from his hometown, South Haven. He didn't mind the ride—it was on the way to the gym. Traffic wasn't too bad, and he liked to unwind in the car after work before he got home. But the ODs were starting to haunt his dreams. Walking into the victim's house, and seeing them white and lifeless, he felt helpless, and he didn't like that feeling. He was starting to think maybe he took the wrong career path; he never gave too much thought to anything else. For as long as he could remember, he wanted to be just like his Pop.

His dad was a proud man, who had lots of friends, and people respected him. John wanted to continue the family name with honor and bravery. But surely times had changed since the days when his dad was a first responder.

Still, he wasn't a quitter. He never quit anything that he really wanted. He would continue to ignore his melancholy feelings. But he couldn't ignore the lack of sleep he was getting lately. Not because he wasn't tired— he was exhausted—but when he closed his eyes, he didn't like what he saw in his head. He could smell that distinctive smell; he knew it anywhere. It smelled a bit like nail polish remover, but worse and it stuck with him. He found if he kept his hands moving, fixing his bike, fixing stuff around the house, building a kennel for Toby out back—anything to not be in his own thoughts—he could manage himself that way.

He managed to get a couple of hours of sleep today, but he awoke suddenly to the sound of the front door shutting, and Toby barking. Julia must have left. Toby always barked when she left. He looked at the time; it was 8 am. *Where is she off to so early?* he thought, and just then he realized he was late for his shift. He was never late. He was upset. Why didn't Julia wake him? He thought maybe she didn't know he had to work today. He usually had a set schedule, but lately he'd been using his sick days. But today he was late. He grabbed a banana and his uniform and jumped in his car.

He jumped on the highway and today traffic bothered him. Seemed like no one was moving; the cars were at a standstill. 'What's going on?' he thought. So, he turned his radio on and he could hear there was an accident up ahead, so he took the next exit—number 5.

He hadn't been off exit 5 in some time. He used to hang out over on this side of town all the time when he was in high school. Tony lived here. Rosebud Lane, number 22. His family lived in a big colonial with a white fence, and Tony still lived there. He was just about to pass the house when he saw an ambulance in the driveway. He recognized the number on the ambulance; it was one of his buddies who drove the type 2 van, Murphy. He pulled over, he wasn't sure if he should just go in, or if he should call Tony, or maybe Murphy. Must be one of his parents, John thought. They were getting older, and John was pretty sure he remembered his father had some health issues. John couldn't remember exactly what it was, maybe his heart, maybe Tony's dad had a heart attack, he thought.

Something came over John and he felt compelled to go inside. He didn't feel that weird, after all, he had been in that house a hundred times before. When they were younger, he remembered playing video games, sleeping over, and hanging out at 22 Rosebud Lane. Plus, he just saw Tony not too long ago.

He walked inside. There was a sound of silence—a chilling feeling that would give him the creeps immediately, right down his spine. He could still feel it if he thought about it for too long. He walked down the foyer and looked up the stairs. He walked to the first landing, and then he heard it. The sound of sorrow. Tony's mom—he would never forget her face, her eyes. She normally was so put together.

She was this little Italian sweet soul, salt of the Earth, stuffed you full until you couldn't move. She normally looked happy, but John could see something was terribly wrong. John took five more steps up and he looked to the right, that's where Tony's room was. Why was everyone in Tony's room? *Did Tony's dad, Anthony, have a heart attack while he was talking to his son?* John thought. But just as John took the last step to the second floor, he saw Anthony hug his wife.

"Tony?" John shouted. Martina turned to John and shook her head and hung it low with tears in her eyes. There were no words, but John understood. John felt tears run down his face, he remembered that grief, that pain, it was all coming back to him, he saw Bo in his head. His stomach felt like it flipped, and he felt like he was going to throw up his banana from earlier. Then he remembered, the last time he saw Tony, he wasn't really all that nice to him. He didn't really pay attention to him. He promised him they would celebrate and go out, smoke a joint, and have some beers when he officially became a paramedic, but he never called Tony; he never tried to set that up.

He felt terrible because there was always this competition between the two. When they were in high school, whether it was on the football field, or with the ladies, he felt like Tony was trying to outdo him, or vice versa. All that seemed so childish now, and he prayed he had a chance to make it all better and repair their long friendship. When the stretcher slowly rolled past, he saw the white sheet was over his face. He felt like he was in slow motion, and he prayed to go back in time. He looked up at Murphy, there were no words. He knew right then and there, Tony was dead.

John never went to work that day. Instead, he found himself in his garage, angry, and sad at the same time. He was not even sure how he passed the hours, but before he knew it Julia was back from Mystic. He heard Toby barking and he heard the door close. He heard her go to the kitchen cabinet and feed Toby biscuits and Tigger treats. He didn't like how Toby packed on ten pounds, at least, since Julia had been around. He thought she spoiled them, and she shouldn't be giving them so many treats. Toby anyway, he didn't really care if Tigger over-ate. He saw the knob turn; he really didn't want to see her. He didn't want to see anyone. He was angry with himself and sad for his friend's family. He could still see Martina's eyes.

He didn't want a kiss hello; he didn't want to be touched. But he also didn't want to tell her why, not now at least. He doesn't even remember what he said, but he knows it made her cry, and he felt bad, but not bad enough to chase after her. He wanted to be alone tonight.

Murphy called John later that evening to check on him, and John found out Tony OD'ed. John threw his fist through the kitchen wall. Tony was so reckless, John thought.

John was just getting out of the shower. The bathroom was steamy. He was so preoccupied in his thoughts he forgot to turn the fan on. The mirror was fogged, so he wiped the steam with his right hand, and he saw what he had done. It was swollen and bruised; it didn't look like his hand at all. It hurt. He could now feel the throbbing. So, he sat on the toilet and wrapped it up. As he sat there in his towel, he thought about Tony. He couldn't believe it. The disbelief was making him so angry. Tony was always careless.

He was the youngest of five boys. *God bless Martina*, he thought. Tony's older brothers were always bailing him out, and Tony was always quick with his words. He got away with everything being the baby of the family, and that was his biggest downfall. Tony thought he was untouchable. But sadly, at just twenty-five, he would find out he wasn't.

John found out later that the family would be keeping this hush hush. They were a big Italian family; Tony had more cousins than John could count. Besides the family, only a few friends would know.

Tony's family made you feel welcome when you were in their home, but you could always sense secrets were around every corner. And some of the stories the father told were downright creepy, but nonetheless they were good people, and they did not deserve this tragedy. John knew he should tell Julia. He knew she would be an appropriate exception to the families wishes, but he would never get the words out, at least not yet.

John woke up early this morning. He got in the shower and thought about where his suit was. It had been a while since he last wore it. He brushed his teeth and looked in the mirror. He couldn't imagine how his parents would feel if he was the one... no, he couldn't think like that, he didn't do drugs. Sure, he drank and smoked a little weed, but he saw what drugs did, and he knew better. He saw the ripple effect poor choices had on family and friends. And John was selfish, but not that selfish. But it wasn't Tony's fault. He thought he was superman—and he kind of was—the super man of his family. John went with a blue tie.

He knew how to tie a tie well, his father taught him when he was young. He kissed Toby goodbye; he needed a little love from his best friend today. Then he left for the funeral. He didn't listen to any music on the way, which was unusual for him. He loved '70s classics, '80s rock, and just about every '90s song—except Sugar Ray, he hated that band. But today he would listen to the sound of his thoughts. He tried to slow them down, but he couldn't, they were racing fast.

He remembered when he first met Tony. He knew one of his older brothers first. His brother worked out at the local gym. John was the check-in clerk there. He loved working at the gym. He got to work out for free, and stare at all the pretty girls, while he looked through sports magazines, and talked to some cool people about some good training tips. John liked to keep in shape; he took care of himself. He was a classy guy.

Christopher was his brother's name and he came to the desk one day and asked if it was ok to bring his little brother, Tony, in the gym, as his guest. John was just finishing making a protein drink, he still had vanilla powder on his hands. He wiped his hands on his pants, and he said, "Ya, man. Don't I know you from school?"

"Ya," Tony said. Antonio was his full name, but everyone called him Tony, even the teachers.

"Oh, just go on in. I was just about done with my shift. You wanna shoot hoops?" John asked.

"Definitely," said Tony. After John washed his hands, he punched out, and changed his sneakers. With his Jordans on he knew he would whip Tony's butt. They played for hours, and from then on they met at the gym in that way for years to come.

John always hated funerals, like everyone, but he felt so awkward at the casket. And he never knew what to say to the family. Wasn't 'my condolences' so generic—where was the soul in it? he thought. Maybe no words were needed. He hugged Martina, she embraced him back. He felt her trembling. He hugged Anthony, Christopher, and all the brothers.

They owned a flooring company, and all five—well four now—brothers worked there. DeCarlo's Flooring they called it—they were proud of their Italian last name. John could understand why they didn't want anyone to know, they didn't want any bad publicity.

Tony's OD was nothing new around here though. There had been a huge opiate crisis for years now, and it seemed like people were dying left and right. John saw it at work and heard it on the news, and it seemed like everyone knew someone who had this problem.

Tony choked on his own throw up while he lied flat in bed. It was said Martina found him. After the funeral, she would head to Italy for a while, where she had plenty of family to help her grieve. She left her husband and her sons behind, but it was understandable.

The smell of the flowers was in the air; there were so many flowers. There were more flowers than people, which was sad. Tony was so popular; the family was well liked in town. Their business was flourishing for years, and they were grateful people for it. Tony deserved a big funeral, he was a fun-loving guy, and John missed him already.

Julia was coming over tonight to get the rest of her stuff. Lately, he wasn't happy with himself, never mind trying to make her happy. She was a complicated woman, and he loved her, but he wished she was stronger. He didn't need her weakness, not ever, but certainly not now. She had to get realistic about her goals. No one was knocking on her apartment door, hunting her down for her books. She thought she had this masterpiece. *Oh really?* he thought. *Why did no one call her back then?* She was determined though, he had to give her that, and that did turn him on about her, but lately he hadn't even gone to bed. Not because he was trying to avoid her, but by then it was just past the point of resolving. He knew he had to work out his own demons, and he didn't want to let her in completely, at least not now.

It was raining, he could smell the rain, that sweet fresh smell—it gave him a sense of melody calmness. He was sad. He didn't really want to break up, but he just needed time apart. He just wanted to be left alone for a while, he wasn't sure how long, and he wasn't sure if he would ever get Julia back, but he knew he had to let her go right now.

He remembered holding her tight, saying goodbye; that last goodbye would haunt him forever, he still remembered hearing her scream to forgive her, and let her stay. And it wasn't about her, and he couldn't make her see that. He knew he was being selfish, but she knew that too. And it never seemed to bother her before. But he didn't want to hurt her; he felt terrible. She turned away so fast. He called to her, "Your box, Julia. These are all your scarves. I put them in this box for you. I counted them. There are thirty scarves in this box." But she kept walking. She walked so fast—he knew he had broken her heart.

There were nights she called him after the breakup, and there were nights he called her. She always knew just when to get him though. It seemed like her timing was always the same. He was just about over her, well, not over her, he probably would never get over her completely. But his days were getting easier, and his nights were getting less cold. He was sleeping a bit more lately and trying to figure out where he went wrong and how to fix his life so he could feel satisfied, or at least lighter, happier.

He liked when she called, but he always knew when she did she was drunk, and that annoyed him, but not enough to deny her. He missed her soft kisses and her radiant skin, and the scarves she put in her hair. He never smelled vanilla like he did on her. He missed her touch. There was no denying it. He loved when she came through the door, even if he could smell the Jack on her breath. He knew that they couldn't keep messing around though—not without attachments.

He knew he didn't want to stop sleeping with her, but he knew she wanted more, and he knew she deserved more. Still, he wasn't ready to let her in. He wasn't ready to let anyone in. He had kept his distance from everyone. He hadn't seen Joe since the funeral, and he wasn't reaching out to any of his buddies lately. He didn't like himself, and he knew he had a long journey of forgiveness ahead before he could love someone again. Still, it was hard to say no when she called.

One day, he was driving home from work. He turned in his driveway and parked in his usual spot. He walked to his mailbox, like he always did. Today, there was a manila envelope in the box, and that was unusual. He looked at who it was from, Julia Jameson. He smiled and opened it quickly, right there in the driveway. He hadn't seen Julia in years, but not a day went by that he didn't think of her beauty.

It was heavy, felt like a book. He slid it out of the envelope and grabbed it with his hand. There it was, two dolphins jumping from the water on the cover, and the most alluring face he had ever seen on the back. He was comforted by her photograph. There was a note in purple ink that read, "You will always be my muse. Much love now and always, J." The cursive J with the little heart next to it; she brightened him up. He wasn't much of a reader, but he took a stab at it. He read the first few pages right there in the driveway, and then he shut the book. He was proud of her, and he hoped she was happy, and he hoped she felt proud of herself too.

It was a nice day to be outside, a little cool, but not too windy. He loved the spring air; he felt a change was coming. He was just about finished with his shift. He had some down time, so he was changing the oil in his car. He was that kind of a guy; he didn't like spending money on things he could do himself. He was at the sink washing the motor oil off his hands when the call came through. The sirens went off.

Damnit, he thought. He was so close to being out the door and on his way home. These days he was finding a little more joy there. He had some house projects that he was finishing up, he felt more motivated, and the projects were helping him get a little more sleep.

He didn't sleep so well last night, though—he woke up in a sweat at 3 am. He thought maybe he was coming down with something. Couple of guys at work were out with the flu, maybe he caught something, he thought. He got to thinking about the last time he was up at 3 am sweating he had been with Julia. He missed her moves, she had a way of wrapping her body around his, and he missed her touch and that angelic face.

He took the thermometer out of his cabinet; he had to search for it. It had been a while since he felt sick like this. He noticed he still had her brush, a bottle of lotion, and contact solution in one of the drawers. He unscrewed the lotion top so he could smell her. He missed the way she smelled, and it reminded him of the way she laughed. He missed the way he felt in her presence.
He always thought of her, but he thought it was strange how intense his feelings were in that moment. He didn't have a temperature, so we went back to sleep, dreaming of Julia, and better days.

He was in the ambulance now, it was just about 4:30 pm, and he heard the call over the radio. He heard the 911 operator say, "It's a 2002 Hondo Civic, green... mint green."

There it was, those words would haunt him forever. His heart sunk to his stomach, and he felt a pit. Like he never had before, worse than the pit Bo left, and that was deep. His palms were sweaty, and it was hard for him to hold the wheel. He knew it was her—down deep in his thoughts—but no, he wouldn't do that. He wouldn't get all in his head. He was still five miles away from the accident. He was cool-headed and hardly ever overreacted. He saw the sirens in his rearview mirror—the cops were racing behind him. There were four fire trucks trying to get through; he heard the trucks honking. Western Haven had a dangerous intersection, and they had been there many times before, but he never felt like this.

He pulled up to the scene. There was the mint green Honda mangled. There she was on the ground. He called to her, "Julia, can you hear me?" He couldn't have been more than twenty-five feet away, but he knew her anywhere. He could see her gorgeous body tangled, her beautiful face cut up. As he got closer he could see glass in her arm, and he could see her scarf around her neck; he loved her neck. He loved when she pulled her hair back and her neck was exposed. And he loved when she tied the scarf around like she was hiding from something.

He ran to her. He told her to be strong, he told her he loved her, and he told her about the scarves.

It was long ago, but he could still remember when he packed up the scarves. He picked them up, one by one.

He studied each one. Some had stripes, some had dots, some were long, and some were short. And at first, he thought it was ridiculous how many there were. He saw a white one, a blue one, a silver one, and then there was the red one.

There was always that one scarf she wore. He loved them all on her, but the red one was special, and for a moment he felt like he was sixteen when times were so much simpler, and he felt free. He longed for the past, and he longed for the future. He knew he needed to make a change. He knew he wanted Julia, but he knew he had so much growing up to do.

That was the last scarf, thirty-one, he counted. He thought, she doesn't need all those scarves, and she wouldn't even know if one was missing. He shuffled through the box. He felt it, satin, soft, silky. He picked out the red scarf, and he held it close to his chest. He took a deep breath and he put it in his pocket, where it would always remain. He would always have a piece of her with him.

He closed the box. He heard the rain starting to come down hard. He liked the sound of the rain, but tonight it sounded like it was roaring with anger. He picked up the box and put it by the door. Julia would be there soon, and he didn't want to forget to give her the scarves, he knew they were special to her, and he was starting to understand why.

Her accident was giving him nightmares, and he couldn't stay away from the hospital. When he was on shift, he would visit on breaks and after work, and on his days off he would sometimes find himself there all day and through the night. He always touched her when he visited, and he would always feel joy and sorrow mixed together. He loved her soft skin. Even in the state she was in, her skin was smooth and velvety.

Her face still radiated beauty, as she laid there peaceful. He would never leave without kissing it. All the hours spent in the hospital were in lonely silence, but he enjoyed the reflection. He wondered how they got here, and how they could love each other so much, but be so distant now? He started to think about how she would ask him to move south to Florida and have a little bungalow down there with a lavender garden. He started to see the greatness in the possibility.

He started to pray. He prayed for a chance to make it right; he prayed for Julia to wake up so he could fix everything. He prayed for Julia's family and friends to have the strength to help her through. And he prayed for himself to find the courage to keep going. He felt such a connection to a higher power, like something came over him at that moment; like an angel touched his shoulders. He shivered and all the sudden, she moved.

She had been in a coma for over a week. But the heart monitor was beating loudly. "Julia?" he said. Her mother had just left the room to talk to the doctors. He knew her surgery and blood transfusions were having negative effects on her body, and he thought the doctors talked about her like she was already gone, and that annoyed him. He knew one doctor from the hospital well, Dr. Onnie. He appreciated her kindness, she was always gentle with her words. It wasn't looking good though, there was no denying that. And even though he felt lonely and distant—he wasn't alone visiting room 22 at Yale Hospital.

Julia had a huge support team; all her family was there constantly. The Bowens, the neighbors she grew playing with in the woods and in her treehouse. They helped her heal when she broke her arm many years ago, and they came in shifts now and were happy to help once again, but they knew this time it was much worse. The Lefkimiatis', who were friends of the family. They were a great big loving family who always brought balloons and food, and plenty of laughs. You know those Greeks there were more than Julia could count.

All of Julia's girlfriends took turns visiting. Friends she hadn't seen in years—old friends from high school and college. Jackie, of course, was there with Tommy and they even brought pictures of Tigger. Between all the family and friends, Julia was never alone. The support and prayers saved her, there was no doubt about that, but on that day John remembered feeling extra close to God. He begged for His help, and he would always be grateful that He delivered.

Everyone knew the road ahead would be long and bumpy, and everyone was doing their best to help Julia through it. Julia was confused about what happened, and it seemed she was in denial; claiming she was never in an accident. She would not talk about it with anyone, not even the doctors could get through to her, so there was a lot of uncertainty in the air. One thing was clear though, John knew he had to make it right with Julia. Almost losing her was just about the worst thing that he had ever gone through, and he knew he never wanted to let her go again.

Part Three: The Awakening

She awoke from what felt like a three-year slumber. Her body felt rested, but her mind was filled with uncertainty, and it left her feeling drained. She remembered that she would never forget that feeling of confusion that fell upon her that day. She was cold and bewildered, and she could not remember anything about the accident, except she knew John was there. Somehow she knew he touched her, even in the state she was in, she knew those hands were on her.

She remembered some wild dreams she had of her childhood. She remembered when her mom and she adopted their first cat. They had named him Oscar. She begged her dad for a cat for months. Her dad wasn't much of a cat person, but he loved to make his daughter happy. She remembered how much joy Oscar brought to her, her mom, and even her dad. She would catch him giving Oscar treats before he left for work and petting him before he went to sleep. Oscar lived a long happy life and she was always thankful for him.

She laid flat on the hospital bed. She felt tears run down her face; she knew it was touch and go for a while. She knew she was near death or at least the closest she had ever been. And she knew she was lucky to make it out of the coma she was in.

She also knew it would be a long recovery, and she could still remember how nice the nurses were. Not as nice as her mom, her very own nurse. Her mom was kind and humble, and she was careful and graceful. Julia knew her mom was scared for her daughter though. She could see it in her eyes. She saw the same fear in her dad and all her family and friends. She was so appreciative and thankful for all their kindness and optimism, and she realized right there in that room, Room 22, even with all the chaos, that was a room full of true love.

She could hear the crackling of the firewood, and she could smell the crisp air. She could feel Toby at her feet, and she was resting on John's body. It seemed like lately they were connected at the hip. She loved how lovable he was being; he couldn't keep his hands off her, and he was so attentive. This was new, and she liked the feeling.

John told her about the accident. He explained how he was there every day, praying, hoping, and wishing. "I knew deep down you would pull through. I knew the love you have and the love you give would persevere." He told her how her friends were there, especially Jackie, Jenny, and Irene. "Irene read romance novels to you. Jenny played her guitar and sang melodies of love and hope. And Jackie told funny stories of when you girls were young." He told her how her mom never left her side. "She slept on the cot every night and only left to use the bathroom."

He told her that before the accident he knew he loved her, but after the accident, he knew he didn't want to live another day without her.

"You want some tea, dear?" John asked kindly.

"Sure," Julia said. He made her a cup of chamomile tea, knowing that was her favorite. And as they watched *When Harry Met Sally*, she could feel a change in the air. She could see a shift in him. He laughed when she laughed. And suddenly it seemed like they were on a different frequency together. She saw something different in his eyes, a softness, a look she never saw before. He placed the tea mug down and he said, "You are my angel. You saved me from myself. I am not perfect, but together we are perfect. I would be honored if you would be my wife."

She was still so sore from the accident, and she wasn't doing much these days. Mostly she was recovering on the couch with Toby and Tigger, and even when they would want her to pet them it hurt her to give them attention. Her arms, her legs, her chest, everything was sore. Of course, she would pet them anyway; she wasn't selfish with her love.

She could not believe what she was hearing, did John just ask for her to marry him? She would be so happy to be Mrs. Julia Brady.

He called Toby over. Julia could see a red scarf around Toby's neck. Toby sat next to John; he always listened to John's commands faithfully. He reached around his neck and untied the red scarf and tied it around Julia's neck. "We want you in our lives, now and forever," he said. He got on his knee and pulled a ring from the red scarf like it was magic and said, "Will you be my wife?"

She screamed with joy, "Yes!" She said it seven more times, "Yes! Yes! Yes! Yes! Yes! Yes! Yes!" She was so happy, all her pain subsided quickly, and she had no cares in the world—she was on cloud nine.

The ring was beautiful; it fit just right on her left index finger. She loved the square diamond and adored the little diamonds surrounding it. She couldn't imagine a better life than the one she had right now. She couldn't wait to show her ring off, to her parents, to the girls.

Jackie would be so jealous, she thought, in a good way, of course.

Julia's birthday was in July, and summer was their favorite season. It was a no brainer; the wedding would be in July.

It was June 2016, twenty years since she sat in his car for the first time. She would never forget that high. She felt like that again—that new, fresh sensation. The celebration of love; she soaked it up.

John and she were on their way to pick out flowers for their wedding in a month. She knew she wanted roses and daisies, and he knew he wanted to make her happy. After hours of talking to the florist and looking through catalogs, they walked outside. It was a beautiful day, the sun was shining bright, and the grass was green. Julia wrapped her white linen summer scarf around her neck and bent down to smell the rose bush. She gently put her nose against the flower and then looked up at John and said, "Have you ever seen such beauty? Have you ever seen something so beautiful grow straight from the ground?"

He looked in her eyes. He could see the sparkle; they were brighter than the diamonds on her finger. He knew he would love her forever, and he said, "Not from the ground, but I sure have seen beauty grow." And he winked at her, and she was captivated. And in that moment, she knew they would get through anything, and she would love him forever.

July 27, 2016 was the happiest day of Julia's life. She was thirty-three and she knew it was a long journey here, but she knew it was worth the ride. All the bumps and the ups and downs brought them here. She finally had her happy ending. She could still remember the way the flowers smelled. They were so fragrant; the smell of berries and clovers were in the air. There were so many flowers, probably more flowers than people, and there were over 300 people, so that's a lot of flowers. Notes of peaches, apricots, and raspberries filled the room while she finished getting ready. She looked in the long mirror and she saw peace and harmony reflect through.

She had baby blue toe polish on for good luck, and she was ready to marry her best friend. She couldn't wait to see him. She heard he chose a purple tie because purple was her favorite color. She knew he would look handsome in purple; he looked handsome in every color.

She heard the music; the violin sounds caressed her ears. She heard the ivory keys playing; she always loved the sound the piano made. She knew it was time to walk. She knew everyone would be watching, and she was nervous. She never liked all eyes on her. She took a deep breath and one last look in the mirror. Her fingernails were French-manicured. Nelly, her old roommate from college, did them perfectly. Nelly did her makeup too. She had a side business in beauty—a sweet girl from Ecuador, and she knew how to make a girl look good.

Julia had a scarf in her hair and pearls that she borrowed from her mom around her neck. She wore a fitted white gown that sparked ever so slightly when she moved. Her heels were new, and her hair was back. She had her neck exposed; she knew John loved that look. And in that moment she was thankful for whomever invented waterproof mascara, they were a genius she thought.

She walked down the aisle with her dad holding her right arm. When she got to the alter her father stopped, turned to her, and whispered in her ear, "I am so proud of you, Julia." There it is was—the confidence she was lacking her whole life. She wouldn't have to search anymore; her parents were proud. Her whole family was there to see it. And she had John waiting for her. He looked so handsome with his purple tie. Toby sat beside him with a purple scarf tied around his furry neck, and he looked handsome too.

She loved weddings, like most people, but she loved the idea that everyone she loved was together to witness, share, and celebrate her and John's everlasting love. Everyone was there: Jenny, Irene, and the Bacardi girls made it. They hadn't all been in the same room in years, but today they were all here. Julia's first job was being a Bacardi girl when she was only eighteen. She made money serving rum to strangers with her girlfriends. She loved that job and remained close with the seven girls she worked with. They all looked beautiful: Jenny, Irene, Juliana, Julie, Trish, and Danielle even came, she was living in Arizona these days, and Julia wasn't sure if she would make it. And of course, Michele; it wasn't a party without her.

Her friends from the South Haven newspaper were there: Brittany, Erica, Tina, Sue, Doreen, and Marge, and they all brought a guest. The Bowens and the Lefkimiatis' were there to celebrate. Hannah and Elaine—her friends from Mystic Aquarium came too.

It was an unforgettable night. Julia danced, let loose, and never felt better. She looked down at her bouquet that was filled with colored roses and daises; she smelled their sweet freshness and took a deep breath in. She turned around and tossed the bouquet over her head. She heard the ladies laughing and the chaos of it all made her smile. Every girl wanted to be the lucky one. But before she turned back to face them, she knew whose hands it was in. Jackie caught it, of course. It was fitting; everyone knew she was next.

The night was just about over when Julia heard the DJ say, "The band is taking a break, and I wanna play 'Sailing' by Christopher Cross for the couple."

She looked up at John who was standing beside her. She said, "Did you do this?"

He knew she loved this song. He whispered in her ear, "You know it! Anything for my sweet love." She headed to the dance floor holding John's hand. He followed her lead. She had heard this song a thousand times before, but tonight she would cry happy tears as he sang the lyrics in her ear.

"You look beautiful tonight," John said after the song was over, and she knew right then and there she would always remember this feeling. He made her feel bliss—a feeling she would crave forever. No one could fulfill this; these two were made for each other.

The next morning, they were getting ready to leave for Hawaii where they would spend their honeymoon. She had plans to ask him to buy a house in Coral Springs, Florida, where his parents lived. She had done some research on her own and she was ready to tell him all about it.

He looked up from his suitcase as he was packing his belongings, and said, "Oh yeah, I forgot to mention. On the way home from Hawaii would you like to stop in Coral Springs?" He smiled and told her to make sure she packed that red bikini.

"What?" She was perplexed. Had she been careless and left some of her notes out? Did he know she was looking? Julia was putting her scarves in her suitcase—all her different scarves. Some had prints, some were plain, some had stripes, and some had dots. She loved them all no matter the shape or size, but he had her attention now.

He walked over and kissed her right ear, took a folded piece of paper out of his pocket, unfolded it and said, "How would you like your new address to be 55 Lavender Lane, Coral Springs, Florida?"

She threw her arms around his neck and kissed him. She was overwhelmed with joy and happiness. She looked in his eyes and said, "You are a dream come true, and the dream keeps getting better and better." She passionately kissed him, and with that they were out the door, headed to Hawaii.

When they got to Gate B to board the plane, the attendant saw them holding hands. He saw the smiles on their faces and the glow of their skin, and he knew they were something special. He said, "I can tell you're one of the lucky couples. I work in an airport, so I know love when I see it."

They smiled more and said, "Thank you. We are lucky, aren't we?"

John squeezed her hand and kissed her cheek. Then the attendant asked, "Where did you two meet?"

They looked at each other, laughed, and then said, "Which time do you want to hear?"

Julia and John's Moon 2019

Acknowledgments:

Thank you to my family and friends for supporting me through this beautiful journey.
Thank you Jacqueline Ruiz for being the best editor – I appreciate all your hard work!

Thank you for reading my story. I hope you enjoyed reading it as much as I enjoyed creating it. Blessings! Forever Grateful
– Jenna, artist and writer

Made in the USA
Middletown, DE
16 March 2019